The Longest Fall

Lee Krinsky

iUniverse, Inc.
New York   Bloomington

The Longest Fall

iUniverse books may be ordered through booksellers or by contacting:

iUniverse
1663 Liberty Drive
Bloomington, IN 47403
www.iuniverse.com
1-800-Authors (1-800-288-4677)

Because of the dynamic nature of the Internet, any Web addresses or links contained in this book may have changed since publication and may no longer be valid. The views expressed in this work are solely those of the author and do not necessarily reflect the views of the publisher, and the publisher hereby disclaims any responsibility for them.

ISBN: 978-0-595-42719-2 (sc)
ISBN: 978-0-595-71908-2 (dj)
ISBN: 978-0-595-87050-9 (ebook)

Library of Congress Control Number: 2009924629

Printed in the United States of America

iUniverse rev. date: 04/01/09

In loving memory of Troy Depass

May 4, 1979 – July 7, 1996

"You have to love what you're doing to go out there and do it when the bleachers are empty."

-Greg Noll

(speaking of Ken Bradshaw in "Da Bull, Life Over the Edge")

SPRING

Spring arrives gently, like a lover unnoticed, waking the soul from its long drunken sleep. "Come, there is work to be done," her voice whispers softly. The harsh afternoon winds diminish, days grow longer and warmer. All that has died comes back to life.

1

JULIAN STARED OUT THE CLASSROOM window. The track gleamed in the afternoon sun. He envisioned himself running around the black oval, breathing hard, pain invading his legs and gut, a nice lead, and one lap away from winning the county title.

"Julian, what does the color red symbolize in *The Catcher in the Rye*?" The teacher interrupted his thoughts.

"Anger," Julian said, not moving his head.

"Very good," the teacher said, continuing his lecture.

Soon the bell rang. Julian walked through the crowds to his locker. He didn't look much a like a runner. Julian wasn't tall or lanky, and his shoulders were a little wider than most of the other distance guys. He was easy to spot with his trademarked shaved head. John was waiting for him at his locker.

"You ready to win?" John asked. He had an athletic physique, and his blue-green eyes, dirty blond hair and slight tan hue to his skin made him strikingly handsome.

Julian looked at him strangely. "I've never seen you so excited about a track meet."

"Track? I'm talking about volleyball intramurals," John said.

The runners were scheduled to play the varsity volleyball team for the intramural championships.

"The county meet is today," Julian replied.

"The bus doesn't leave till 4:30," John said. "We have plenty of time."

Reluctantly, Julian agreed.

Boy's volleyball intramurals at Atlantic were not the usual intramurals. They were attended by large crowds of students and had great social significance. Winning would surely increase an Atlantic student's popularity; possibly help them get in with the girl of their choice.

That year, the runners had created quite a buzz, destroying the other teams. They had one victory left, though: the varsity volleyball team. It would be quite a challenge. They were the underdogs, but the crowd was in their favor. The kids were going nuts.

The trash talking began as soon as the game started, and things didn't look good for the runners. The volleyball team had a player who was 6'5" and a ferocious spiker. Still, the runners were gifted athletes, good at almost any sport. They kept their cool and played hard.

The runners took the lead and soon it was point game. It was Julian's turn to serve. He tossed the ball high in the air—and at that exact moment—Coach Dower burst into the gym.

"Get off the court!" Dower's voice exploded like a cannon.

Julian's serve slammed into the net.

"The state qualifying meet is today and you're playing volleyball?" The runners scattered towards the locker rooms. Julian tried not to make eye contact as he jogged past Dower.

"I expected more from you, Julian," Dower said.

His words stung.

The county, or state qualifying meet was held at Mitchell Field, near Nassau Coliseum. It was a beautiful track, soft to the touch and well lit if the meet went late. It could get quite windy on the track, as it was very open, but that day the wind was light and high temperature was about 70 degrees. It would be a great afternoon for running.

There were three teams that could win the county title: Oceanside, Uniondale and Irvington. Oceanside had a near unstoppable distance team, while Uniondale owned the sprints and field events. Irvington High had a well rounded team. Julian did believe Atlantic had a shot at winning, but only if everyone performed at their best. More importantly, he hoped to win the two-mile or at least qualify for the state meet—which meant finishing in the top three positions.

The two-mile was the first event. There were several runners in the race who had beat Julian that spring. However, he had not yet faced the best runner that season. His name was Shawn Gunther, a junior from Irvington. On paper, Gunther was the fastest runner in the county. The problem was, he ran those times at invitationals, and always seemed to be hurt during the big meets like counties.

Boom!

The race went out slow, which was not a good thing for Julian. He was more toughness than speed, and won his races by wearing out his opponents, not by sprinting at the end. He knew Gunther had a blistering kick, and if he was near him with a lap or two to go it would be tough to win.

After the first three laps, the pack began to spread out. A small group of six runners near the front separated off, with Gunther leading them. Julian stayed right behind him.

Still, the pace was not very fast. When they came through the mile mark, Dower shouted, "Stay right with them, Julian!"

Gunther began a surge on the fifth lap. The front pack started to thin a little. Julian and two Oceanside runners stayed just behind Gunther.

With a lap and a half to go, Gunther took off. Julian and the Oceanside guys attempted to follow.

Julian let one Oceanside runner pass him but held the other off. His legs and gut were burning.

"Come on, Julian!" Dower yelled.

On the backstretch, the second Oceanside runner passed Julian. Julian followed him along the final turn, and then kicked hard on the final stretch. He exploded with all his strength and might, but could not catch him. In fact, he was nearly passed by another runner.

The Atlantic runners fared no better in the mile and 800 meters, with no one qualifying for states or even in a position to score the team any points. Atlantic's final shot to have any distance runners qualify came down to the last race of the day—the 4x800.

Dower slammed the baton into John's chest. "Bonds, you're leading off. And don't go out too fast."

John, a junior, was new to the team. He had a tremendous amount of natural talent and kept getting better as the year progressed.

Boom!

John exploded off the line. At the end of the first turn, he moved to the front, taking a 10-foot lead on the next runner, and remained there for the entire first lap.

"Slow down, Bonds!" Dower screamed. Then he turned away from the track and yelled to no one in particular, "He went out too fast!"

John led through the next lap too. An Irvington runner tried to pass him on the backstretch, but John was fresh and was able to hold him off easily.

John handed off the baton to Simon. Simon was the slowest runner on the relay, but he was consistent. He retained the lead for most of his first lap, but was overtaken by an Irvington runner towards the end, and then by an Oceanside runner.

"Stay with them!" Dower screamed.

Simon followed the two runners, but did not gain and both

runners managed to put some more ground on him before he handed off.

Pedro shot off the line like a missile. He had tremendous speed, but didn't always use his head. He overtook the Oceanside runner on the turn, and then quickly passed the Irvington runner.

"What is he doing?" Dower screamed.

Pedro had not even completed the first lap before he started to fall back. Before long, the Irvington runner passed him, and the Oceanside runner passed him soon afterwards. Pedro did all he could to hold his position on the next lap, but two other runners passed him before he handed off to Julian.

Julian darted out and fought hard, pushing towards the leaders. But as hard as he fought, deep down he knew the real race was between Irvington and Oceanside.

Julian managed to pass two runners for fourth, and a good time on his split. Still, it was the first time in Dower's career that he did not have at least one distance runner qualify for the state meet.

Dower instructed the four to do a brief cool down before the team left. They jogged in silence. Julian was tired and angry, and just wanted to go home and sleep.

As they finished up, they passed the Irvington team heading towards their bus. Irvington was the wealthier, bordering town to Atlantic. The schools were arch rivals.

"Nice race, girls!" one of the Irvington boys yelled.

Pedro flashed his middle finger at him. He was Latino with dark hair and eyes.

"Better get used to this!" another tall, stocky boy shouted as he mooned them. "This is all you're going to be seeing from now on!"

Though skinny and shorter than the average height, Pedro charged him and the two struggled. The kid raised his fist to hit Pedro, but John intercepted him, checking the boy hard, knocking him to the ground. Simon was a scrapper too, and started swinging wildly. Julian tried to break it up but soon found himself blocking punches and delivering his own.

Parents began yelling and soon several adults rushed over and broke up the fight. Dower and the Irvington coach noticed the commotion and stepped in. Both sides told their own stories. Since neither coach saw the initial push or shove, the coaches used their own judgment for disciplinary actions.

Dower was livid. He told the boys to get on the bus. Julian expected a scolding, but Dower didn't say anything. In fact, he was eerily quiet the entire bus ride home. This made Julian even more nervous.

The locker room was quiet when Dower came in. He was an average height man with thick shoulders and arms. He was almost 60, but looked younger.

Dower had started coaching in the late 60's, when he was not much older than the seniors. Within a decade, he managed to take an unknown team and create a nationally recognized team that dominated the local and state competition. The team even had its own showcase displaying plaques and awards from prestigious meets like the Penn Relays, Milrose Games and Nationals. Two team alumni had even made the Olympic team.

Dower was now at the end of his career. Things had only changed in the last few years. The amount of talent had declined, and the team was just barely winning the big meets. That school year the team had lost its first county championship title in over ten years.

Dower walked to the back wall, where newspaper clippings he had saved or photocopied were taped. Some of the articles were of his great teams from the 70s and 80s. He looked over the articles as if it was the first time he had ever seen them.

An awkward silence prevailed and the only noise Julian could hear inside the locker room was the leaky faucet.

After what seemed a long time, Dower walked to the front of the locker room and turned towards the runners. His words came unhurried. "Never in my thirty years of coaching have I witnessed anything like today." Then he started to pace. "But this is not just about today. This has been going on all year. Not a single one of you has taken it seriously. And today you got what you deserved." Dower stopped pacing. "Do you like being mocked by the other teams?" His voice started to rise. "None of you have to be here, you know. This isn't mandatory." He paused a moment, then exploded, "But if all you want to do is goof off, then go play intramurals!" The words came crashing out like a tidal wave and his face was flushed.

Dower resumed pacing, and then stopped at the back wall again to look at the articles. A few of the runners exchanged nervous glances.

When he turned around, there was a change in Dower's tone. "This team has enormous potential—*enormous*. If you want to waste it, that's fine." He paused briefly then roared, "But not on my time!" He made sure to stare each of them in the eye. "If you're not going to take this sport seriously, stay home this fall."

With that, he left.

Pedro broke the silence first. "That freshman's having a party tomorrow night, right?"

No one responded.

"What's the matter with you guys? It's not like someone died," Pedro reasoned.

"Some of us are actually mad because we didn't make the state meet, Pedro," Julian said with a wry face.

"What? You think I don't care?" Pedro defended. "I care, but I'm not gonna sit at home and cry about it."

"Me neither," John said. "Life's too short."

"You guys are unbelievable," Julian said, grabbing his bag. He stormed out.

Julian did not walk straight home. He walked out to the track and sat on the bleachers. It was Friday evening and the place was desolate. The sun had set, but yellow light still soared from the horizon. Julian peered over at the track. It was old and in need of repair or replacement. He thought about all the great runners that had competed there. It had a certain aura. Julian thought of the suffering and toil that had taken place there. He wondered what it was like back when the legacy began, and what those runners knew that he and his teammates did not.

He could not help from feeling that he had let his brethren down. Atlantic was a team that was once feared. Now they were mocked.

He was frustrated, but in his heart, he knew he had not given it his best effort. Dower was right; the team goofed around more than they took things seriously. They were playing soccer and basketball when they should have been running. And it was not just that one day, it was the entire school year.

2

Atlantic High School was composed of various cliques. The two main ones were the jocks and the G's. The jocks were mostly athletes and cheerleaders—somewhat of a popular crowd. The jocks dressed conservatively in collared shirts, baseball caps and brown shoes. The G's were rougher looking with their hair slicked back, leather jackets and tight clothing, and the girls in that bunch wore less clothing. The two groups did not like each other and rarely interacted.

In addition to those two main groups, there were the freaks, the straight-edge crew, and the nerds. These were no ordinary nerds though; it was rumored that they partied hard and studied little.

The runners were considered a clique too, but the label might not have been the most appropriate. One could recognize a member of the other cliques immediately by their attire, but not the runners. Julian's hippie-like sweaters, necklaces, and jeans made him a standout in Atlantic. John was a t-shirt, jeans and whatever-he-could-steal-from-Julian's-closet kind of guy. Brett had a plethora of flannels and other hand-me-downs from his older brother, which, with his rugged good looks and muscular build, looked cool on him. Pedro wore cheap imitations of high-end fashion clothing—attire he believed would surely attract the opposite sex. Usually though, it only brought on ridicule. Simon preferred to wear the same t-shirt for the entire week. At times, he would put a flannel or sweater over it. He looked older than the other teammates with his rusty colored beard.

The social scene at Atlantic functioned more like a college than a high school. There were great jock parties nearly every weekend. The seniors would try to find a younger classman to take advantage of, one who could not foresee the damages his house would incur. If they couldn't find a vacant house, they would direct the kids to one of the local school yards or the Atlantic bleachers. During winter, the more hardcore seniors and party goers could be found complete with wool hats, scarves and gloves. They really were a dedicated bunch.

One of the freshmen on the team was having a party that night. It was supposed to be just a "track party," but Brett and Pedro told the entire school so a large crowd was expected.

Julian was lying on his bed, wearing sweatpants and a t-shirt, watching TV when he heard the doorbell ring. Seconds later, John burst into his room.

"What are you doing?" John asked.

"It's called watching TV."

"You're not going to the party?" John asked, nearly exasperated.

"Nope."

"Shauna's coming and so is her friend *who wants you*."

"They'll be other nights."

John paced around the room manically, unsure of what to say next to convince him. The doorbell rang again.

'Who'd you invite here?" Julian asked.

"No one." John said.

Moments later, Alex and Lowell, two sophomores on the team entered his room. Alex was short and pale-looking, while Lowell towered awkwardly over him with darker features.

"What are you two dorks doing here?" John asked.

"Julian invited us," Alex said, a little perturbed.

It was then that Julian remembered making plans with the lower classman earlier that week. Julian sat up on his bed. He figured it would do him some good to go out and get his mind off things.

When they arrived at the party, the house was already packed. They went into the backyard.

"Hey, girls!" the notorious Brett O'Conner shouted. He was an Irish kid with short dirty blond, almost brown, hair and blue eyes. Brett stood at 6'2" and looked old enough to be in college. He was a runner, too—or had been until he was kicked off the team the previous week. After losing the team the relay, Brett threw the baton. The act itself wasn't so bad, but the baton ricocheted off a fence and hit a referee in the groin.

Brett turned to Julian. "Well, did you guys qualify or what?"

"Nah, we got killed," Julian replied.

"But we did get into a fight with Irvington," John said.

"No way!" Brett shouted. "Darn, the one meet I don't go to."

"You could have shown up," Julian said.

"Then I would have had to run," Brett said.

Julian shook his head and walked away. He wasn't in much of a mood to party. Luckily, most of the kids had no idea about the meet earlier in the day so he didn't have to answer any questions.

John's girlfriend showed up with a large group of friends. She was from Irvington High School. The Irvington girls were a little more refined, but got a real kick out of the Atlantic boys because they were a little rough around the edges. Brett and Pedro attacked her friends like vultures.

A little later, Julian noticed Simon wander off into the backyard behind the house where the party was. Simon was normally a loner and a quiet kid who didn't speak much, but this night he seemed even more withdrawn and low in spirits.

There were several bushes separating the two yards, but Julian found a pass. He spotted Simon sitting on one of the lawn chairs at the end of the backyard, brooding.

Julian took a seat near him. "You like this house better, champ?"

Simon shrugged.

"I know how you feel," Julian said.

"I didn't beat any of my sophomore times, Julian."

"I know, Si, we all had a horrible year."

Simon shook his head. "I'm done, man."

"What?"

"I'm quitting, Julian."

"Look, Si, you were hurt all cross country season."

"During track I was fine and none of my times got better."

"None of us took this year seriously." Julian paused for a moment. "We slacked off all season. You know it's true."

Simon stared at the ground.

Next thing they knew, someone starting to urinate on the other side of bushes.

"Hey, we're sitting here," Julian called.

The stream stopped.

"Who's that?" a voice called.

"Julian, who's that?"

It was then that John walked through a bush. "What are you guys doing back here?" John said zipping his fly.

"Talking," Julian said.

"Oh, yeah? About what?" John said.

"Running," Simon replied gravely.

"I thought we were done."

"Listen, John," Julian said, "the fun and games are over. We have one more chance and that's it. This is our last year. We make our mark now or never."

"Forget track," Simon said. "Cross country is what it is all about, anyway."

"John, you're going to be good this season—real good. And we are going to take back that title."

The lights in the house went on.

"Let's get out of here," Julian suggested.

Towards the end of the night, Brett and a few other big guys took all the furniture out, put it in the backyard, and a huge dance floor was constructed out of what used to be the boy's living room. They found some 70s disco music, pumped it up and, lo and behold: A dance party was created.

But soon after, there was a large commotion in the backyard. Apparently, the G's had shown up, and the Jocks told them they were not allowed in. A large fight erupted and, soon after, someone threw a chair from the backyard through the living room window.

Not long after, the police arrived. Julian gathered his friends and got them out of there. The runner always had an advantage when dealing with trouble: They could run fast, and run for long.

They walked back towards Simon's house, which was the designated house for late-night sleepovers. Simon had a huge furnished basement that could easily sleep the entire team. The best part was the back entrance, where they could easily sneak in and out.

As they walked, Julian suddenly started making whooping sounds and yelled, "Atlantic cross country, 1996! Retake the title!"

Soon, the others joined in, making noises. Then, Brett and Pedro climbed up on cars and continued chanting as they approached a corner with a four-way "Stop" sign. As they marched across the street, it became obvious that a car heading in their direction wasn't stopping.

The driver slammed on his brakes and the black Mustang skidded towards them. The runners didn't even have time to react—but luckily, the car finally stopped just a few feet before them.

Brett glared through the windshield and kicked the bumper as hard as he could. "Watch where you're going, moron!"

The driver's side door opened and out walked Frankie Cussado.

Cussado was one of the most feared kids in Atlantic school. He was not big, but he was crazy, and always traveled with at least two large friends or "bodyguards." This time he had three large kids with him.

"Who just kicked my car?" yelled Cussado.

"I did," Brett admitted.

Cussado looked at Brett, but walked over to Julian instead and gave him a hard stare. Julian had over an inch and ten pounds on Cussado, who wasn't very big. He knew he could rip him to shreds and matched Cussado's stare with a stony look of his own.

"Better tell your friend to shut up, runner," Cussado warned.

"Why don't you tell me?" Brett said.

"Let's teach these runners a lesson," one of Cussado's friends shouted.

Cussado stared at them for awhile, and then finally cracked a smile. "You guys are lucky I'm on probation. But you better watch your backs. Especially you, O'conner."

"Whatever," Brett said.

Cussado and his buddies got back in the car, the doors slammed shut and the car peeled away.

"Wimps!" Pedro shouted at them.

There was a long silence between the group.

"We would have killed those guys," Lowell said.

"Shut up," Brett responded.

The runners all looked at each other and tension quickly broke into laughter.

Simon passed out the second they reached his house, but some of the others decided they were hungry, and decided to make a frozen pizza. While the pizza was cooking, they all passed out.

Julian woke up and smelled smoke. He went upstairs, opened

the oven and black smoke rushed out. Julian quickly shut off the oven.

John and Brett came up. "Pizza ready or what?"

"You nearly burned the house down," Julian complained. "We have to air this place out or the fire alarm is gonna go off."

At that moment, it went off.

It was right above Brett's head. He jumped up and instead of shutting it off, managed to rip the entire unit off the wall. John and Brett burst into laugher, doing their best to contain it.

"Shut up, idiots," Julian whispered. He opened the screen door and led the others outside.

The three plopped down on the grass. They laughed loudly.

"What are we gonna do now?" Julian asked between laughs.

"Don't worry, I'll take care of it," Brett told him.

3

JULIAN AND JOHN WERE OUTSIDE shooting hoops in his driveway. Julian threw him the ball.

John paused. "Why do you think those guys didn't try to fight us last night?"

"Because they didn't outnumber us."

"True, they only like it when it's ten on one." John shot the ball.

Julian grabbed the rebound. "Some of those other guys are tough, but Cussado only likes to pick on small kids."

"They were big, but I think we could have easily taken them."

"Whatever. It doesn't matter." Julian shot a three-pointer and made it in. "I'm glad it didn't happen. They could have had weapons on them or in the car. If we'd fought them and won they'd just come back with more kids or weapons. You don't win with those kids, John, they have no honor." Julian took another three-pointer and got it in.

"Honor?"

"If a real man wants to fight another man, he does it one on one. He doesn't get ten of his best friends to do the job…or a weapon."

"I'd go one on one with any of them."

Julian shook his head. "Not with those guys. They hide in groups or behind weapons. But the bottom line is, it all comes down to fear."

"Yeah, they're a bunch of wuss's."

As they were finishing up their game, they noticed Simon jogging towards them. He stopped when he reached the sidewalk. "What's up, guys?"

"Hey," Julian and John replied and returned to their game.

"Do you guys know what happened to my fire alarm last night?" Simon asked.

John's next shot air-balled.

"You know what, Si?" Julian asked nonchalantly, "I've heard Lowell sleepwalks."

Julian looked to John for back-up.

"I thought I heard something…late," John added.

Simon rubbed his head. "Well, I guess that would explain it."

"Explain what?" John asked.

"Somehow the fire alarm fell off the wall. And someone put it in the freezer."

John turned his back and smothered his chuckle. Julian was a better actor.

"I'm grounded for two weeks and have to buy a new one."

"You should go talk to Lowell about this," Julian said.

"Lowell? I figured it was Brett or Pedro."

"Nah, I bet Lowell was the culprit," Julian said.

"Yeah?" Simon asked.

"I heard that he once drove his parents' car while sleepwalking," John jumped in. Julian shot him a stare.

"Really?" Simon said.

"That's right," John replied.

"Don't let Lowell lie to you either," Julian added. "He can be very crafty."

"OK," Simon said as he jogged away. "I'll get it out of him."

"And don't be afraid to use force," John yelled out to him.

They waited until Simon turned the corner to fall on the ground in laughter. A car beeped as they lay on the blacktop.

"Get off the driveway before I run you two over," Julian's sister shouted.

They rolled onto the grass. It was the last time the team would sleep over at Simon's house.

4

Usually on Sundays, Julian would take a long run—a cleansing ritual to get the lactic acid out of his system. This Sunday, Jimmy Docile or Doc, as the others called him, asked Julian to run with him.

Doc was arguably the best distance runner to ever come from Atlantic. He had seven state meet victories in high school and a twelfth place finish at the national cross country championships—and it was rumored he had a virus that day. In college he had two NCAA wins under his belt—and he still had one year left.

Not only was he one of the fastest distance runners to ever come from Atlantic, but Doc was also one of the smartest. He was the valedictorian of his class and had encyclopedic knowledge on everything from training to Eastern religion. He was nicknamed Doc before he had even chosen to attend medical school, and would often be found philosophizing with others.

Although he came dressed to run, Doc always insisted they meet in the locker room. Julian walked to the back of the locker room and did a few stretches while he waited. As he faced the wall, he noticed a posted article that he hadn't seen before, "*Cross*

Country State Qualifying Meet, New York Tech, 1991. Jimmy Docile, Atlantic 15:49, Jack Iron, Atlantic 15:59, Shane Johnson, Utica 16:02, Jamie Fairchild, Seneca 16:08, Scott Tildon, Atlantic 16:22. Team scores. Atlantic 35, Seneca 83 and Middletown 112."

Julian considered the slowest time in the article, 16:22, and compared it to his best time, 16:50. While he was the first man on the present team, he would have been fourth man on that 1991 team.

"Ready to go, kid?" Doc asked. His presence broke Julian from his mental turmoil.

The sight of Doc always made Julian smile. Supposedly, a man in peak physical conditioning, Doc looked as if he was deathly sick most times. He was skinny to the point of being nearly emaciated, pale because he avoided the sun at all costs unless running, and was always in need of a shave. Though he received stylish new clothes from his coach and friends within the industry, he preferred the old T-shirts he received as prizes in the many races he won. The only thing he really cared about were his sneakers—which are important to any runner who averages a hundred miles a week.

"I'm sure you saw the paper," Julian told Doc a few minutes into the run.

"Yeah, you guys were slaughtered. I thought the two-mile was your event."

"I was out-kicked on the last 200."

"The last 200? What about the other 1.9 miles of the race?"

Julian took the hint.

"Let me tell you a little fact of life, J.," Doc continued a mile later. "People don't always get what they deserve, they get what they *believe* they deserve."

"I'm not sure I understand, Doc."

"Our beliefs largely define us. And, often times, what we believe limits our potential."

Julian nodded his head.

"So if you're in great shape and you still have a lot of doubts about your ability, there's good chance you'll act on those negative thoughts."

"So I psyched myself out?"

"Maybe. I wasn't there and I can't get into your head. But the point I am trying to make is this: a guy who *isn't* in the best shape can win with the right attitude and mental toughness. At a certain point, a race becomes much more mental than physical."

Julian admitted, "I don't think any of us believed we could win."

They ran the next few miles in silence. Finally, Julian spoke again. "Doc, do you think I have a shot at winning the state meet next fall?"

"Doesn't matter what I think, that's a matter between your feet and the ground."

"Anyone ever tell you you're hard to talk to?" Julian asked.

"That's why I spend most of my time running."

Another mile later, Doc said, "You want the real secret, Julian? What the greatest distance runners have all known."

Julian nodded.

"There is no secret."

Doc chucked. Julian was not amused.

"All kidding aside, Julian here it is: To become the best, you must train harder than anyone else. Training hard is not enough. Every good runner trains hard, but to become the best you must constantly push yourself past your limits. You must constantly strive to break your threshold. And this is a battle that never ends."

After mile twelve, Doc dropped him off at the school.

"How far you going?" Julian asked.

"Another four or five."

Julian smiled.

"Take a day or two off before you start your summer training, kid." Doc suggested. "Have fun, go to the movies, hang out with your friends—try being a normal kid!"

Julian walked away, grumbling, "I hate the movies."

5

THE MOST DEFINING DAY OF Julian's running career was when he beat Oceanside senior, James Sutton. It was earlier that year, during the fall cross country season. It was a warm day and the race was at Bethpage State Park.

Bethpage was a mostly flat course and began on a large polo field. The runners went across that field, and then disappeared on a series of trails for over two miles.

Most people thought it was an easy course because it was flat, but Julian would always argue otherwise. Because there was no crowd, the runner was alone for most of the race. It was a real mental battle.

James Sutton was a fast and talented runner. But Julian was tough, and cross country was his sport. They went head-to-head in the back woods for most of the course—almost as if they were running as friends. But there was silence, and Julian was giving all he could to break Sutton. He wanted to prove that he was tougher—not just for himself and his own ego, but for his team. Atlantic was always the best cross country team in the county.

Julian overtook Sutton near the end of the course. With a grueling pace—pushing it on every stride—he moved ahead of him. Julian never looked back—and there was no reason to. He gave it all he had.

As the season went on, things changed. Injury plagued some of the runners and they began to slack off. Then Julian choked in the county meet, losing to Sutton, and several other runners he had beaten during the season. The team lost the title, which was the first time in over a decade.

Things fell apart after they lost the county title. The pressure was off and no one expected much after that—not even from themselves. The winter and spring seasons were even worse. Sutton and the Oceanside team dominated within the county, and Sutton did not lose one race. The Atlantic team was crushed meet after meet, and soon, none of them began to take it seriously.

No one pushed Julian during workouts, and he was not pushing his teammates either. They played basketball, soccer or video games when they were supposed to be doing their long runs.

Julian took Doc's advice and took a few days off. He hated taking days off—it felt unnatural. But it was necessary to make him stronger and to replete his body. It was on those days that he ruminated on his horrible performance that year.

His first day back, Julian had only jogged a few miles, and the next day, he went five. But on the third day, he could not control himself, his legs felt fresh, but he felt restless. Waves of energy pulsed through Julian's veins. The anger and frustration burned at him. He knew of only one thing to do to purge himself: run. And run hard.

Julian jogged to the track. He stopped for a moment, centered himself, and then took off. Julian ran a lap exactly as he would in a race—not a fast, out of control pace, but a solid pace that would put him on track for a fast time. On the second lap, he could already feel the burn in his legs. Julian knew it was going to be a rough one.

The third lap was slower and the pain spread from his legs to his gut. His arms also began to tire. Julian tried to pick it up a little on the fourth, but found it difficult. This made him furious and he took it out on his body. On the fifth lap, he surged. The pain increased, but he didn't feel like he was going any faster, and it just made him angrier. Julian pushed harder and harder. Then, on the sixth lap, he realized his form was out of control and he was wasting too much energy. He needed to relax if he wanted to finish the right way.

As he entered the seventh lap, the pain was excruciating. His legs and stomach felt like they were being impaled by knives and his body felt heavy, like he was wearing an iron vest. Julian wanted to slow down, but didn't. He pushed harder, but not as wildly as before, relaxing his arms and breathing in as much air as possible. Then a feeling of tranquility came over him: He felt as if he was not alone. The Atlantic runners of the past were running with him and cheering him on. Deep shivers ran through his frame, and he pumped his arms and moved his legs as fast as he could. Halfway through the last lap, his breathing began to spasm. Julian felt as if he was about to lose consciousness, but held on. He pumped his arms wildly around the final turn as if reeling in a shark, and pulled himself towards the finish.

The final stretch was a maniacal spasm of body movements. He ran through the finish and collapsed. Julian briefly lost consciousness and, when he came to, it took him a few seconds to remember where he was and what he was doing there.

Julian remained still for a moment as he tried to catch his breath with massive heaves. When he finally stood up, his legs were shaking, and he felt hot and dizzy. It was then that the feeling of awe came over him—all the discomfort was replaced with a feeling of ecstasy. In that moment, Julian had a great insight: he controlled his destiny. If he wanted to be a great runner it was up to him.

Julian jogged home a new man. He understood that his goals could not be accomplished in one night, but he had the answers he needed. He was going to win the state meet that fall and he would train harder than any runner in the state that summer.

6

MONDAY JULIAN WENT TO DOWER'S office to speak with him. Dower was sitting at his desk going over some papers.

"I'm going to win the state meet this fall."

Dower stopped working and looked up.

"And so is the team," Julian continued.

"Go on."

"I'm going to train harder than any other runner in state. And so is the team."

Dower took off his glasses and leaned back in his chair. "Julian, take a look around my office." He pointed to the many trophies and plaques on the wall. "I've been around this sport for a long time. Longer than you've been on this earth. I've produced more championship runners and teams than any other coach in New York State. The one thing that I've learned in all my years is that you cannot create desire. A great coach can motivate his runners, but, ultimately, they have to want it. Julian, you—and many of your teammates—have real, natural ability. But talent means nothing in this sport—it's nothing without dedication and the hard work necessary to cultivate it."

Julian nodded.

"I don't question your dedication as much as your teammates. Sure, we have a bunch of guys who like to run, but we're not a team. A team is only created when there's a bond, when each runner is willing to make a sacrifice for the sake of the team. Sadly, we do not have that."

"How do I make the other guys change?" Julian asked.

"The best way I know is to change yourself."

Julian nodded, stood up and started to leave.

"I'm the last person to tell you it's impossible, Julian. I just want you to understand the commitment it takes to win the game at that level. Start back gradually, give your body a few weeks to acclimate," Dower suggested. "Train hard, but train smart. Our team is too shallow to have anyone get hurt."

7

JOHN, BRETT, SIMON AND JULIAN grew up together and were always great friends. They were all good athletes as well. When they were younger, they could often be found playing some kind of sport on any given day or evening.

When John was in junior high, his parents got divorced. It was then he found out his father had been seeing another woman. His mother would stay out late, or all night, and he soon learned how to care for himself. Soon, he lost all interest in sports and his friends. John fell in with a tougher crowd in high school, and started smoking cigarettes and drinking alcohol.

John played one season of football his freshman year at Atlantic. He stood out as a fast, powerful runner whenever he got the ball. The lacrosse coaches knew of his athletic ability and tried to recruit him. But it was no use; they were unable reach or reckon with him. John was a recluse and didn't care about anything or anyone. Some of the G's asked him to be part of their crew, but John pledged allegiance to no one and was soon seen as an outcast to them, too.

The summer before his junior year, he met Shauna. She was beautiful and had a thing for bad boys. There was only one problem: she was already seeing someone at Irvington. And the boy had a reputation for being a tough kid. But that did not stop John, who had little fear of anyone or anything at the time.

During the first week of school that year, John found out the boy and some of his friends had planned to jump him after school. John went into the track locker room right after school to hide out, but someone spotted him. Soon, John was surrounded by a group of Irvington kids. The word got out to the G's that there was going to be a fight and the locker room was filled with kids.

Even though the G's didn't like John, they despised the Irvington kids even more and did not want them on their turf. John asked for a fair fight and they backed him up.

John's first punch nearly knocked the boy off his feet. He hit him with two more and the boy was on the ground. Then John kicked him in the ribs for good measure. The other kids were going nuts. At that point, another Irvington kid attacked John and chaos ensued.

Dower and the football coaches heard the commotion and rushed in. They knew the difference between the athletes and the troublemakers and tried to grab the latter as they fled. Even though John got away, the coaches knew his face, and the next day he was called to the principal's office.

While the principal wasn't a huge supporter of school athletics, the dean was. Luckily, the dean—who was also the wrestling coach—handled all disciplinary matters. Surprisingly, John was given a plea deal: If he picked one sport and stayed with it all season, he would be absolved of all punishment. He would be given one day to make his decision.

The coaches really wanted him for football, lacrosse or even wrestling. Most of the G's played football, and he had no real interest in wrestling or lacrosse. The coaches nearly laughed when he chose cross country. Even Dower was surprised.

Dower didn't know the boy well, but had a long talk with him after the meeting. While Dower could easily spot a troublemaker, he could also easily spot talent. He was very honest with John and told him about running. He let him know how much hard work was involved and what it really took: guts. He wasn't sure John had it in him, but thought he might do well as a sprinter because he had natural speed. If John stayed on the team for the year, Dower promised he would help him get into college. But he would have to stop smoking.

John started cross country. Julian and the others took him right in. He didn't like it much at first, but he soon saw rapid progress as did the others. By the end of the season, he was on the varsity, beating most of the seniors. Dower and Julian convinced him to stay on for track.

John stopped smoking and ditched the remnants of his old crowd for Julian and his teammates. He ran a 4:45 mile indoors, but it was not until the outdoor season that his natural prowess showed. John ran a 4:35 mile and a 1:59 half-mile at the state qualifiers.

It was a phenomenon, really. At first, John didn't know what to make of it, but soon came to terms with it, having no other choice. Each day between 10:01 and 10:14—smack in the middle of third period—John would have the urge to have an intense bowel movement. Initially, it was no big deal. John wasn't a shy individual; he'd raise his hand and out he went. Since he liked to use the bathroom in the track locker room, where he had a private stall and could use his own soft toilet paper, his trips were long. Soon, it started to cause a disturbance and cause the class to laugh. One day, the teacher informed John he wanted to see him after class.

The teacher was convinced John was leaving class to smoke cigarettes. John told the man he was on the cross country team, but his argument proved futile. John tried one final plea on the maxim, "When you gotta go, you gotta go." Still, as the behavior persisted, he was met with a series of detention appointments.

The next day, John was late to class. And the next day too.

Then the detention began. On his third day late to cross country practice, Dower called him out in front of the team. John explained the saga with a straight face. Dower had no idea what he had gotten himself into. The team rolled with laughter and, on this rare occasion, Dower was at a loss for words.

The strangest part happened the following day, though. The teacher pulled John over before class and told him if he needed to go he could just walk out. At first, John likened the event to divine intervention. But after telling the others the story, he was informed about the privileges of being a varsity athlete.

John thought, *How great the life of the young runner is—a private bathroom, soft toilet paper and a get-out-of-detention card. What more could a young man ask for?*

After his bathroom break that day, John strolled back to class. His 5'10 frame, maroon hat with wisps of dirty blond hair coming out the sides, green t-shirt stolen from Julian that read *Go Pre*, made him stand out in the hallway crowd. Dower made him out from a mile away and he stopped him at the end of the hallway.

"Hey, Coach," John said.

"Where are you going?"

"To class."

"Which class?"

"English."

Dower studied him. "1:59 half-mile at the qualifiers." Dower nodded. "We just might make something of you yet, Bonds."

John smiled.

"You should start your summer training soon," Dower said as he started to walk away. Then he stopped a moment. "And get a hair cut, would ya?"

8

THE LAST WEEK OF SCHOOL, Julian had been training by himself or with Simon. He was surprised to see John, Alex and Lowell in the locker room.

Julian grinned. "I didn't know there were volleyball intramurals today."

"There isn't," Alex said.

"So you guys are here to run?" Julian asked, somewhat surprised.

"I'm not going far," John said.

Julian smirked. "Don't worry, I've got the perfect route."

The others frowned.

The route they were on was named "The Bridge Run". It started at Atlantic school and went all the way to the Jones Beach trail along the Wantagh Parkway. The trail went all the way to Jones Beach, but usually the team only went to the first or second bridge.

It was hot so Julian set a controlled pace. As he ran, he began to talk with the others. "I'm going to win the state meet next year and so is the team."

"States?" Simon asked.

"*Yes, States.*"

"How are we going to win states? We didn't even win counties last year," Simon said.

"We're going to have a much better team this year."

"But it's the same team," Alex pointed out.

"Each of us is going to run over 500 miles this summer."

"I don't think I've run 500 miles in my entire life," John said.

Just as they approached the bridge, something peculiar happened—Julian stopped running. The others looked at him strangely.

"What's going on?" Simon asked.

Julian looked out over the water. "You guys have to understand something." He started to take off his sneakers and socks.

The others watched him, confused.

Then Julian took off his shirt and jumped up on the railing. "Anyone can be great at this sport." He turned and jumped off the railing, falling 25 feet into the water.

The others ran to look over the railing. Julian soon resurfaced, smiling, treading water. Suddenly, a noise sounded from the other direction. A speed boat was coming.

"Julian, watch out!" John screamed, but Julian was already under water.

The yellow speed boat passed almost directly over where he had been. The others waited nervously for him to come up.

John climbed over the railing and was ready to leap fully clothed when he saw Julian treading water at the far end of the bridge.

"I'm going after him," John pretended, taking his sneakers and shirt off.

Simon had no clue of the prank and jumped with his sneakers still on.

"I'll get help!" Alex shouted. "Come on, Lowell."

Simon soon realized it was a prank. The three exited the water on the other side of the bridge. They couldn't stop laughing as they watched Alex and Lowell try to stop motorists. Each kept driving past them no mater how frantically they waved their arms.

Alex and Lowell noticed them approaching.

"Real funny, guys. Real funny," Alex said.

When they returned to school, a group of jocks was standing in front of the school. "I thought track was over," One of them yelled.

"It's never over." John joked.

Julian thought about it as he walked home. *John meant it as a joke, but how right he was.* Running did not end when school was over. The runners could not just take the summer off. No, they had three months to improve. County and state champions were made over the summer. *So much could happen in three months.*

Summer

The hazy days stood long until the sun bent over the horizon, with the cascade of pastel colors no longer as sharp as in the winter months. The air became moist and swollen, and weekdays meshed into weekends. School was out and summer was in full swing.

9

Julian could hear the old boat coming from a mile away. Brett had a '79 Buick that had been headed for the junkyard when his father took it in. He originally fixed it for Brett's older brother Bruce, but Brett had recently inherited it when Bruce bought a new car.

Brett pulled up. John and Pedro jumped in the front with Brett while Julian, Simon, Lowell and Alex piled in the back of the car.

There was traffic on the parkway, which was as common to Long Island as the summer humidity. Brett had one tape in the car, a Zeppelin mix that was actually stuck in the player.

Alex strained to open his window, which was broken. "Can you put on the AC?"

"How about you walk the rest of the way?" Brett answered.

The beach was packed. The runners made their way towards the ocean, zigzagging around oily men with huge muscles and women in skimpy bikinis, large white coolers, sheets with stereos, and holes dug by kids.

Midway to the water, Alex put down his side of Brett's huge cooler and asked, "Can we stop here?"

Lowell dropped his side of the cooler too.

"Hey!" Brett shouted. "Watch what you're doing. I've got valuables in there. Pick it up. We're going down by the water."

Brett finally stopped about fifty feet from the water's edge, near a group of attractive young girls. "Perfect," he said as he took his shirt off.

Julian stared at Brett's stomach, a layer of fat covering what used to be ripped abdominal muscles.

"What are you staring at?" Brett asked.

"Have you been running at all?"

Brett was visibly annoyed at the question. "I had to run away from your sister's boyfriend the other day after he caught me in bed with her." He winked at John.

"You guys want any lotion?" Alex asked as he put the thick paste on his white torso.

Brett turned to him and said, "No, I want to get a tan."

"Too much sun isn't good for you," Alex informed him.

"Too much? You're whiter than my ass."

Brett took a football out of his bag, tossed the ball to John, and began to jog towards the ocean. "Throw me a pass."

John stepped back, cocked his arm and launched the ball far past the ocean's edge. Brett hurdled over the incoming waves and leapt, grabbing the ball with one hand in display of his athletic prowess. He brought it to his body and fell into the water.

Julian shook his head. "Probably the first time he's run all summer."

They spend the day swimming, playing ball and hitting on the girls near them. Brett managed to get a number, but as usual, Pedro struck out.

Julian, Alex and John were running home. Lowell asked Brett for a ride since he had to be home.

"Sure," Brett told him in an unusually pleasant manner. But as Lowell opened the back door, Pedro stopped him.

"What are you doing?" Lowell asked.

"I said you could have a ride, I didn't say you could sit in the back seat."

Lowell stared at him, confused. Brett popped the trunk.

"Get in," Pedro called.

Brett passed the group on the way out. Then there was a loud noise from the trunk as the car went over a speed bump.

"Is he going to be all right in there?" Alex asked Julian.

Julian nodded. "He'll be fine."

10

JULIAN WORKED AS A REGISTER boy at the local King Kullen, a job he had started his freshman year. As he progressed, and his parents saw that the sport might pay for his college rather than all the hours he logged in the store, they allowed him to take the school months off and work only during the summer.

John took it upon himself that summer to get a job at the deli near his house. At first, he just stocked soda, washed dishes and swept. But soon the owners realized he was capable of more and had him working the grill and making sandwiches. Though he had to be there early each morning, he liked the job and they let him take home beer when he wanted. He ran with Julian in the evenings.

Brett worked for his father, who was a steamfitter. After work, he would usually camp out on the couch until dinner. Brett ignored Julian's phone calls to run as best he could, but he could not ignore his mother. She was a strong-willed woman, and even though her sons were large and intimidating to others, his mother ran the house. She would literally pull Brett outside by his ear. Sometimes Brett actually ran, other times he would stop at a friend's house around the corner to play video games. When he ran without stopping, it wasn't far—usually no more than five miles, but he ran fast with his long stride.

Simon was a camp counselor. His original plan was to run twice a day—once before camp and once after. But his plan wasn't working out so well. Simon had trouble waking up in the morning, and when he did get up early enough to get a run in, he would be tired all day and have to take a nap after camp. His naps lasted anywhere from one to eight hours. Sometimes, he woke in time to join Julian and John for a run, but it was usually dark by then. It made Simon's mother sick, but he could not be argued with. Though quiet, he was determined.

Pedro worked the hardest of all of them. His father and uncle owned a small construction company. Pedro worked long days, sometimes six days a week. It wasn't uncommon for him to put in more than 50 hours in a week. The work was physically exhausting, but it paid very well. It was the only way he was allowed to participate in school sports year round. Sometimes he would squeeze in a run or two during the week, but usually he just did one or two long runs on the weekend.

Lowell worked at the same camp as Simon, though Simon preferred to ignore him most of the day. Alex didn't work, but waited for Lowell to run each day after camp. Sometimes they joined Julian and John.

Julian made sure to call them weekly, to make sure they were keeping up with their running. He liked to run in the mornings when the air was still cool, but it was easier for him to train with the others in the late afternoon. He and John ran each night around sunset when it would cool slightly. Julian insisted they run no less than an hour, though at times John was reluctant and wanted to make it shorter. Soon, they created a normal route. It was eight and a half miles. The route began and ended going west and it went along most of the perimeter of Atlantic. They started the loop around sunset and when they finished it was usually dark.

Sometimes, they ran at a blistering pace without speaking.

Other times, they ran slower, talking more. After they'd run, Julian's mother would have huge dinners ready for them. John ate there so frequently she included him on her shopping list.

It was July 4th and the boys started their run early as they had a party to attend later. Julian was quiet and had a determination in his every step—as if some silent ghost was chasing him. They came down the final street, galloping like shadow horses and the scintillating lights were just starting to appear.

11

LOVE SEEMED AS SWEET AS summer rain to the runner—warm, satisfying and refreshing all at once. It was the cool beach sand, the blue afterglow following a sunset, and the morning birds' harmonious chirps.

John was fast asleep, buried in his girlfriend Shauna's huge leather sofa.

"Wake up," she whispered, blowing lightly into his ear. She was a pretty girl with blond hair and blue eyes.

John opened his eyes, looking confused. "What time is it?"

"4:30."

"I have to be at Julian's."

"I know, that's why I—"

John kissed her before she could finish the sentence. They kissed for a while before he got up to leave. At the door, he turned back to look at her. She was kneeling where he had been sleeping on the couch. She stared at him with a long face, like a hurt puppy.

Every Tuesday night the runners went to Sunken Meadow State Park on the north shore of Long Island. Before each Meadow run everyone met at Gary's house. Gary was the leader of a local running team called the Milers.

Gary was an alumnus from Atlantic as were most of the Milers. Gary ran for Atlantic in the late '70s and had been a standout runner on a standout team. He was known for his outrageous personality and antics. Now he mostly ran marathons and had five wins in major races.

A large group of men were assembled in front of Gary's house when Julian and John arrived. Julian introduced John to Gary.

Gary spoke like a drill sergeant. "How far you guys been running?"

"About eight a day," Julian answered.

"Take any days off a week?"

"One day ever other week."

"Don't take any more than two for the rest of the summer. That goes for you too, John. See you boys there."

After he walked away, John looked over at Julian. "What is that guy on?"

"Life," Julian replied.

A deep voice sounded as a powerful hand came down on Julian's shoulder. "Hey, look who's here!"

It was Bruce, Brett's older brother. Bruce was shorter than Brett by a few inches, but he was about as wide. He was also one of he best all-around athletes to ever graduate from Atlantic, standing out in football, wrestling, discus, and shot-put. Bruce wasn't a real distance runner, but came down to keep in shape. He was best friends with Doc, and seeing the two of them together was quite a site as Bruce's forearms were larger than Doc's legs.

"And if it isn't little Johnny Boy!" Bruce shouted.

"I heard you were running, but I still don't believe it."

"Running? I'm here for the garage sale," John joked.

"You always had that sense of humor, Bonds," Bruce said, grabbing John around the neck and putting him in a headlock. Then he let him go and grinned. "You guys come with me and Doc. Brett, go find a ride."

The Meadow was far, but it did not take long to get there the way the Miler's drove. Many of them were cops, who drove the parkways like it was the Autobahn.

Sunken Meadow State Park was Julian's favorite place to run on the island. The Meadow was on the north shore and bordered the Sound. There were marshes along parts of the trail at points. Sometimes, the boys went swimming in the Sound after a run.

Still, the purpose of the trip was training. Many cross country courses had hills, but the streets of Atlantic were flat. The meadow course had hills, and one hill in particular that stood out was "Cardiac." Cardiac was a steep hill planted smack in the middle of the course. It was a hill that could make or break runners—a hill so steep it could rob their will. Yet, if the runner stayed tough, he could also greatly increase his position on this hill.

Dower was already there when the others arrived. A teen-aged boy was standing beside him.

"This is Benji. He'll be a freshman in the fall," Dower said.

Julian walked over and shook his hand. Benji looked more like a junior. He was shy but Julian was able to make conversation with him.

Gary disrobed to show an Olympic physique, hidden only by a small pair of bright orange running shorts. Some of the boys laughed at his outfit, but made sure he didn't notice.

"Andiamos!" Gary commanded, which meant, "Let's go!" in Italian.

The group ran the course twice. Eventually, they built up to three loops, and each week the pace got quicker. Gary was meticulous about his workouts, constantly looking at his watch and position on the course.

When the group was finished, they were greeted with a truck filled with water and beer courtesy of Dower. "Beer for the men, water for the boys," he said, patting the runners on their backs.

Gary greeted Dower. "Looks like you got yourself a couple of runners here, Coach."

"Where?" Dower said sarcastically.

Brett nonchalantly tried to grab a beer. He walked a few feet with it before Dower noticed.

"Put it back," Dower said sternly.

Brett gave him a dirty look and complied.

Dower came over to where Julian and the others were standing and looked them over for a moment. "O'Conner, would you tell your mom to buy you some new sneakers?" He pointed to the legendary hole-ridden, once-white, dark grey sneakers that Brett bought his freshman year. Julian and some of the others swore those sneakers were what gave the track locker its odor.

"So, has everyone been doing what they're supposed to?"

"Every single night," Brett shouted, humping an imaginary set of hips in front of him.

Dower was not amused. "Anyone been doing anything other than playing with themselves?"

12

ATLANTIC WAS ON LONG ISLAND, New York. Long Island was a meshwork of towns of different classes packed closely together. Overall, it was a heavily populated and developed area, ripe with shopping malls and stores. Along any main road, myriad signs unfolded for miles at a time, as did fast-food chains and brand name stores.

Atlantic was mostly a blue collar town filled with down to earth people. It had a small-town feel to it with parks and lakes where one could slip away from the development, and many family-owned businesses. It was a town where people still left their doors unlocked, visited their local pub, and talked to their neighbors.

To the south of Atlantic was Irvington, one of the wealthiest towns on the island. The streets were lined with great mansions and decorated with expensive cars. Julian knew many of the kids who lived there. Some of them he liked, but others were spoiled and snotty. They thought themselves above the Atlantic kids and referred to the Atlantic kids as "dirt bags." And because of this vast class difference, there had always been a large rivalry between the two schools. Sometimes, there were fights, but not often since the Atlantic kids were much tougher. Most of the rivalry played out in sports. Both schools had excellent teams and gave each other great competition, though Atlantic traditionally had better teams in most sports.

Seaport was the town west of Atlantic and was one of the poorer towns, inhabited mostly by minorities. The town looked run down in parts and the difference from the wealthier parts of Long Island was vast. Though Seaport bordered Atlantic, there was no interaction between both towns. There were rumors that Atlantic kids would be jumped or robbed if they found their way into Seaport.

Julian did not notice these vast differences until he started running. Only then did he physically make his way into this bordering town and get a feel for it. Yes, it was a different world than Atlantic, but, strangely, he always felt comfortable there. In fact, his favorite route went through parts of that town.

Julian knew there were small-minded individuals in his town that stereotyped these areas and types of people. This always bothered him because he was brought up in a household where that type of behavior was simply unacceptable. He listened to the other kids' racial jokes and did not laugh. Instead, they angered him.

On the track, everyone was equal. Hazing and teasing happened with kids, but Dower had a zero-tolerance policy with racism. One strike and you were gone. Hatred was simply unacceptable.

Though Seaport looked different on the outside, Julian imagined these neighbors were very similar in many ways; the parents had dreams for their kids, the kids had ambition and goals. The local merchants ran their businesses the same as Atlantic merchants.

Julian would run down their streets, and some of them would stare. He wondered what it would be like to grow up in their town. And he couldn't help wondering, what his neighbors thought of him, and his town.

13

OVER THE SUMMER, DOWER WOULD write three letters to the boys. Julian waited in joyful anticipation for the letters to arrive. The tone was blunt and urgent, and Julian often felt like the letter was personally written for him, though it was photocopied.

> Boys,
> Greetings! I hope this letter finds you well rested and enjoying the summer.
>
> Last year was quite a disappointment for track and cross country. I think we can have a great fall though. We have talent, but we must be willing to work hard. If you are not willing to work hard, don't join us.
>
> It will be us, Oceanside and Irvington fending for the county title. We are not as deep as we used to be. We need 10 runners in great shape, not 7. Julian, make sure to call all the boys. You other guys, call

your friends—and don't be afraid to bring in a new recruit. We need bodies.

You should all have started your summer training by now. Varsity runners should be running as close to an hour a day as possible. For the newcomers, a half hour is all you need. Brett and Pedro, don't do what you did last summer. (Alex and Lowell, same goes for you.)

Every Tuesday, we meet at Sunken Meadow. If you are serious about making States, I expect to see you there. Also, enclosed is an application for cross country camp. I cannot stress how important camp is. You must all go.

See you at the Meadow,
Coach D

P.S. Running 2x a day can't hurt.

14

IT WASN'T UNTIL THE MIDDLE of July that Julian saw the changes happening inside of him. His endurance had exploded. When he ran, Julian reached a place where pain and fatigue meant nothing to him; his body just seemed to ask for more. Julian's stride became effortless. He moved fluid-like and felt he was exerting no energy as he streamed along. He had never run the kind of mileage he was doing—and felt so great. Every week he and Dower went over his log and Dower offered suggestions.

Sometimes, he would even lift weights after a run. It was hard dragging John with him, but once he was there, John didn't complain and pushed him. Julian also found a diet in *Runner's World* and stuck to it the best he could. He also took Doc's suggestion and worked on his mind as much as his body. He visualized himself being in the lead and winning.

Julian put up inspirational quotes and his favorite Nike ads all over his room. He watched movies like *Rocky*, *Field of Dreams*, *The Natural*, and *Fire on the Track*. He would invite the other team members over. Usually, it was only the under classmen who joined him.

Julian understood the changes going on inside of him and

felt it was his time. There was no more fear or nervousness. There was only pain—and pain was his friend. He knew it was only temporary and never lasted beyond the finish.

There was no more losing. Julian was winning now, all the time, even in his dreams.

15

THAT NIGHT, AS JOHN AND Julian ran, they started to talk about how good John would be if he had joined the team as a freshman. John was modest about it, even uncertain, but Julian was convinced John would be the best man on the team. In fact, he felt it was time to find out. Slowly, he started to pick up the pace.

It wasn't an outright race, but Julian did want to find out what John was made of and see if he could break him. Julian kept the conversation going to not make it seem so obvious. But soon the conversation stopped.

They both went hard, fighting for the lead. Before a turn in the road, John passed him. Julian followed. He knew he had the better endurance and it was just a matter of time before John slowed down. John didn't slow much, but Julian caught up to him, and then took the lead.

Julian pushed the pace hard, but couldn't gain much ground on John. Then, with just under a mile to go, John abruptly passed him. Julian tried to follow but could not keep up. Still, he stayed calm, imagining John would slow again. But he didn't, and Julian lost sight of John as he neared his house.

John was sitting on his front porch, chuckling, when Julian finished.

"What happened, Champ?" John asked.

"Cramp." Julian lied.

"Sure," John said, letting the word linger.

Julian walked into the house.

"Hey, what about dinner?" John asked.

"What about it?" Julian asked, shutting the door.

Though Julian let his competitive spirit get the better of him for a minute, he was not mad at John. In fact, he was happy. He needed to push John to show his competitive spirit, and Julian needed someone to push him, too.

16

WHILE RUNNING AT THE MEADOW, John had a strange experience. He lost all sense of his body and felt as if he were weightless, floating over the trail and running without any effort. Soon, he had only the faintest sense he was actually moving, then lost all sense of self.

It was as if he were watching the entire event from some distant vantage point. There was no one there to propel his body anymore. All notions of separateness evaporated and there was no distinction between John, the trail and the woods. And in this consummate place there was no John, had never been. There was also no time, places and limits nor words and names for things.

Then, suddenly, he was back, running with the group with only a faint sense of his body. He was simply some entity breathing hard under the dusk sky. Soon after the group finished, things felt back to normal.

During the car ride home, John didn't say much, still trying to figure out what had happened. He wondered, *Was this the so-called mystical running high? No, it couldn't have been.* He was pretty sure he knew what a running high was, and the experience he had was not really a feeling of pleasure, anyway. It was as if something huge had enveloped him.

"Julian?"

"Yeah?"

John paused for a moment.

"What?" Julian asked.

"Never mind," John said.

"What's the matter?"

John then noticed something in Julian's eyes. The presence had come back. It was as if they were connected somehow.

"What?" Julian asked, smiling at him.

"Never mind," John replied. When he got out of the car, he quickly shut the door and walked away.

"You're so darn touchy these days," Julian said jokingly from the open window.

John walked into his house, wondering if Julian knew.

17

A FEW NIGHTS LATER, Doc called Julian. "You and John meet me at the track."

"Why are we going to the track?"

"To train," Doc said firmly.

Later on, the three met.

"I thought the coach didn't want us here," Julian said.

"We're running intervals?" John asked, disgusted.

Doc grinned. "Don't worry, we're not doing intervals, but we are doing a workout...a mind workout, that is."

"You runnin' with us?" Julian asked Doc.

"I already ran today. For now, I'll just hang out with my watch."

Doc started them off. He did not say anything the first mile and just called off times. During the second mile, Doc started yelling out strange things to them.

"What are you saying to yourself as you run?"

"What is he talking about?" John asked.

"Trust him," Julian suggested. "There's a method to his madness."

When they came through, Doc asked, "The inner chatter… is it positive or is it negative?"

"Dude, this guy is a freak," John said.

But Julian started to see his point.

After mile three, Doc jumped on the track. "What are you telling yourself now?"

John twisted up his face, but Julian started to understand the purpose of the exercise.

He saw how his mind chattered during the training. How it wandered, how it wanted to be in other places. How it alerted him to small pains in his body.

"What is the picture you see in your mind?" Doc asked. "Are you here, on the track or are you somewhere else?" Doc stopped with a mile to go.

Then, on the last mile, he shouted, "How great do you feel? Can you picture yourself in the lead?"

As Julian and John crossed the finish line, Doc looked at his watch. "Not bad gentlemen. Not bad at all."

Doc did the cool down with them and said, "We are what we think about, so training your mind is as important as training your body." Doc smiled. "We used to come to the track all the time in the summer. And we would run the naked mile."

John and Julian exchanged looks.

"Er…that was a long time ago," Doc added.

18

THERE WAS A LARGE GROUP at the Meadow that day. The new college season was close and a lot of the runners came down to get a workout in on the hills.

It started at the end of the first loop, when one of the new college guys started to push the pace. He was an arrogant kid who taunted some of the other runners—even the Milers. The season was right around the corner and everyone was anxious. Soon a few other guys went with him and a small group partitioned itself away from the main—a race had broken out. But there was a strict no-racing policy at the Meadow enforced by Gary at all times.

"Fall back!" Gary yelled.

The rest of the group ignored him, with the arrogant kid calling, "This is America! I can do whatever I want."

Some of the Milers joined the front pack and started racing too.

"Get back here!" Gary screamed.

Nobody budged. Julian knew Gary would not alter his pace or training schedule even if God himself appeared and asked politely. Doc moved up in an attempt to mediate, but it was useless.

When the two groups came alongside the parking lot at the end of the second loop, Dower did not look pleased. "No racing!" He shouted. "Stay with the group!"

Again, it was futile. And soon, Julian caught the fever. On the next loop, he started a burst towards the front pack with some of his teammates following.

Not long after, people started dropping off. Brett was first, then one of the older Milers, and then one of the college guys. On the second loop, Dower didn't say anything. He just stood there with crossed arms, looking vexed.

While Gary was the biggest dog there, Doc was by far the best runner. Doc clearly understood the no-racing policy, but had not yet done his hard run that week. For his last mile and a half, he decided he would teach the arrogant boy a lesson and ran him into the ground. The boy attempted to keep up, but was a disgusting sight as he lost all form. By the end, Doc had managed to put almost twenty seconds on him, finishing up the nine mile run with a 4:30 mile.

John, Julian and Pedro managed to stay with the front group until Cardiac. First Pedro fell back, then Julian. John was the only one who was able to finish with them.

The first thing Gary did after he completed his three loops was banish the arrogant ringleader from ever training with him or at the Meadow again. After that, he scolded the college guys and some of his own men as well.

When his runners caught their breath, Dower walked over and put his hand on John's shoulder. "Looks like we could have a new number one man."

19

EVERY SUMMER THE MILER'S PUT on a fundraising race. Since they put on the race, none of them ran. Dower always encouraged the Atlantic runners to participate, though it was not mandatory.

It was a 5K run on the streets of Atlantic. Everyone was running, except Pedro because he had to work.

Julian was not a fan of the course. It was run on the streets and brutal with no sun coverage on the hot summer morning.

Dower stared at Brett, who was wearing a dark blue t-shirt, lacrosse shorts and his disgusting sneakers instead of a thin tank top and running shorts.

"Brett, that's what you're racing in?" Dower shook his head.

"You said it was just a workout," Brett responded.

"Yes, meaning you didn't have to wear racing sneakers. You're going to be hot in that shirt. Go see if I have a tank top in my trunk." Dower handed him the keys.

Several minute later the team was met with a surprise: Several Irvington runners jogged by, including Shawn Gunther.

"What are they doing here?" Dower asked.

"It is America, coach," the assistant coach said.

A surge of adrenaline released through Julian's body. His heart beat ferociously as it had in the biggest races of his life. He would now have a chance to truly test himself against one of the best. He didn't care what Dower said about using the race as a time trial. Shawn Gunther was in for the race of his life.

The teams locked stares before the race stated. There was no trash talking though. Julian was all about business.

Boom!

There were some good runners in the race, but there were also some foolish runners who went out way too fast. Julian used his head and kept near Gunther.

Near the end of the first mile, the pack evened out. The teams were nearly head-to-head, spread out across the road. There was a clock at the mile mark, where Dower stood with Gary.

The lead pack of high school runners went by in 5:10. Dower stood with his arms crossed and didn't say a word.

Halfway into the race, Gunther surged. Julian went with him. He was hot, but his body felt good. Julian pushed as hard he could. He did not want Gunther to move ahead of him. Julian held him off.

With a mile to go, Gunther made another attempt to pass, but Julian wouldn't have it. He did not want to give Gunther an ounce of control.

But Gunther pulled slightly ahead. Julian began having flashbacks from the spring championship meet: *The sun beat down hard on his head, his arms were heavy, and his legs and stomach burned. He was being passed by an Oceanside runner and getting out-kicked on the final stretch. The Oceanside runner was just out of reach, and each stride moved Julian farther and farther away.*

The memory passed and a new thought arose in Julian's head: *The past has no relevance on this race.* An electric current traveled down his spine. Julian's memories lost relevance in that present moment. He gathered control of his pain and fatigue, and started driving forward. He gained ground steadily until he finally caught Gunther.

They were both head-to-head as they came down the final stretch. Julian ran with all his energy and focused his thoughts. Julian pressed with everything he had. He moved ahead, and finished first.

John was third, only 12 seconds behind them. An Irvington runner beat Brett, and another beat Simon, but the Atlantic team had five runners finish before the Irvington team had four. If it were a real cross country race they would have destroyed them.

Dower's anger had subsided and he had sort of a curious grin on his face after the race.

"Well, looks like we finally have a team," the assistant coach said.

"Indeed, we do," Dower nodded. "Indeed, we do."

After the race, everyone went over to Gary's for his annual post race barbeque. When Gary did anything, he went all out; there was a copious amount of meat that had been marinating for days, along with homemade salads, and ice chest after ice chest filled with cold beer. Dower kept a watchful eye on the beer coolers at all times.

There was much excitement at the barbeque, but still Dower did not want the boys to get too excited.

He cautioned them, "One of Irvington's best runners was not there today."

"But Pedro wasn't there," Alex countered.

"Still," Dower said, "They and Oceanside will be a huge threat. You all must focus on your training and not let this race get to your heads. A lot can happen from now to November."

Julian had to leave early to help his aunt move some furniture, but he made sure to get enough to eat before he left. He said his goodbyes.

"See you at the party later," Brett shouted. "We'll get hammered." He paused as Dower shot him a stern look. "Happy. We'll get very happy."

The others laughed, but Dower just rolled his eyes.

The parents of the girl who was hosting the huge party that night were away for two weeks. John and Brett drank a lot, and the night went by in a blur.

The next morning, John woke up shirtless on a couch without a clue where he was or how he had gotten there. The clock read 5:35 a.m. Finally, he realized he was in Simon's basement. He looked around and saw Brett and some of the others, but he did not see Julian. Then he remembered he had to be at work at 6:00 a.m.

John's hangover did not set in fully until about 8 a.m. and the day dragged by. He was supposed to work a double, but his boss let him leave early since business was slow and he could tell John was hurting. John went home and fell right to sleep.

John woke up at 7:45 p.m. It was late and he wondered if he had missed Julian's call. John checked his messages, but there were none. He put on a t-shirt and sneakers, and as he was about to leave for Julian's, the phone rang. The next thing John knew, the room was spinning. He dropped the phone and rushed out the front door. Then John dashed down the street, heading east.

Sweat poured from his brow and his shirt slowly began to get soaked. Great pressure came into his skull, John felt a heat he could not escape. Then a great thirst raged in him and intense nausea set in. The road started to slope and the light around him dimmed. John stumbled a few times before he collapsed.

A man coming home from work found John face down on his lawn and immediately called 911. Inside the ambulance, the EMTs thought his name was Julian since that was what John kept repeating. Later, when he came around fully, he was identified at the hospital. The nurse was surprised to learn he was from Atlantic since he had been found nearly seven miles away from his house.

20

AFTER THE BARBECUE, JULIAN HAD gone to his aunt's house to help her move. He finished just after dark and headed back to Atlantic, looking forward to the party. Julian drove slowly, reflecting on the race earlier in the day. He saw a car traveling towards him in the opposite lane at a great speed. As the car reached a bend in the road, a truck shot out from a side street, cutting the quick-moving vehicle off. The car veered into Julian's lane, misjudging the distance between the two cars. They hit head on at full speed.

The collision sounded like a bomb exploding. The speeding driver died on impact, but Julian survived the actual crash. He fought for his life with the same courage and grit he had brought to all other battles. The doctors said they had never seen anything like it—his internal organs were badly damaged and he had lost so much blood. Yet, it was as if his heart would not stop beating.

John woke in the hospital early the next morning. His mom was beside him, sleeping in a chair. Her eyes opened. The first thing she did was stand up and embrace him in a long hug—something they had not done in a long time.

"Where am I?" John asked, slightly disoriented.

"In the hospital," his mother replied. "Someone found you unconscious on their lawn and called for an ambulance. You must have run there."

Suddenly frustrated, John said, "I wanna go home. Can I go now?"

John had only suffered dehydration and shock. The doctors told him to rest and stay hydrated the next few days. His head was still pounding and he felt nauseated so he opened the hospital window to get some fresh air. The sun had recently risen and the sky was exploding with oranges, reds, and yellows. The sight made him furious. He felt things should not be so beautiful during such a horrible time. John felt as if God was mocking him.

When they reached the house John went right to bed. It was a long time before he fell asleep. He tossed and turned for hours, seeing images of Julian's face and hearing the sound of his voice.

John's room was darker when he woke up. In the first few seconds of being conscious, he had forgotten what happened. Soon, the horrible realization set in. He sat up on the bed and didn't move for a long time. Then he decided to take a shower.

When he was done, he went into the kitchen. There was a note on the counter:

> *John,*
> *Had to go to work. There is a team meeting at Si-*
> *mon's house at 7:30. I will meet you there later. I left*
> *a sandwich for you in the fridge.*
>
> *Love,*
> *Mom*

John looked at the clock. It read 7:33. He opened the fridge and took out the sandwich, turkey with mayonnaise, and took a bite. The cold lump of meat slowly moved down his throat. He put the sandwich back in the fridge.

John did not want to go to Simon's house so he went to his room, turned on the radio, and lay on the bed for awhile. He didn't want to see or talk to anyone. Soon, he realized he could not sit in that room by himself all night either. He needed fresh air.

The sun had just set. A pool of shallow, yellow light loomed above the horizon, and shadow-like clouds sat in the dark blue sky. John started to feel better as he walked. When he reached Simon's house, he stopped. He assumed whatever was going on there was going to be horrible. But then, as if of their own accord, his legs carried him forward.

Simon's mother was talking to the large group of kids and parents in the backyard when John entered. She paused a moment as he took one of the empty seats towards the back and everyone turned to look at him. Then she continued, "I want you all to know I'm here if any of you need to talk."

Next, Dower stood up to address everyone. His eyes were a little swollen, like he had cried recently. It was the first time John had ever seen him the least bit vulnerable. "We have suffered a great loss, but Julian will live in our hearts forever. No words can describe what we are feeling right now nor comfort us enough. But we are a family and have each other. We will get through this together." He paused briefly before continuing. "You must all keep running. I cannot stress how important this is. Each of you has my number. Feel free to call me at any time if you want to talk."

Then Simon stood up. "Right now, I don't know what to say...I think..." Tears streamed down his cheeks. He tried to speak again but started crying. His mom and dad came to his side.

John walked out of the backyard. Across the street from Simon's house was the elementary school where John, Julian, Simon, and Brett had gone as children. John walked across the field to the empty playground, sat on one of the little swings and pushed off.

Brett's mother saw John walk out. But as she stood to follow him, Bruce stopped her. "I'll go talk to him, Mom."

Bruce was older than Brett by four years. He was nearly 250 pounds of solid muscle—an intimidating sight of a man. When angered, he could be ferocious, but normally, he was a nice easygoing, even tender guy.

John saw Bruce as he approached. He tried sit down on the swing next to John's, but got stuck. They both smirked, but finally Bruce managed to squeeze his large frame into the small seat.

"I know things look real bad right now, John, but it's going to be all right," Bruce said.

John took a long time to respond. "What kind of life is this, Bruce? One day everything is perfect and the next moment your life turns to hell. Your best friend is ripped away without so much as a goodbye."

Bruce took a deep breath and nodded his head. "John, it's hard to understand these things when they happen. It's hard to see from our perspective that there may be a greater purpose or plan to every event."

John's rage welled up inside him. "So this happened for a reason?"

"Look, John" Bruce said calmly, "there's a lot I can't explain about life, but there is one thing I am sure of: We all loved Julian like a brother." Bruce paused and took a deep breath. "But we have other brothers in that backyard too, and they need us."

"What am I supposed to do? Go cry with them?"

"You're stronger than those guys, John. Brett isn't as tough as he looks. He was crying in bed all day."

"Come on, let's go back." He stood up and waited patiently. John stayed put for a while before he rose. Then Bruce put one of his enormous arms around him and led him back to the house.

They went through the front door to the kitchen, where some of the team mothers were drinking coffee and talking. The mothers shifted and made room for John at the table.

"Have you eaten anything today?" Bruce's mother asked.

John shook his head. Then she grabbed a plate and, from a pot on the stove, scooped two huge spoonfuls of spaghetti and meatballs onto it. She poured him a huge glass of milk. "Eat this, John. It will make you feel better."

John ate in silence slowly as the mothers watched him. John went back outside when he was done, but he didn't speak to anyone.

That night, he slept a little better, but even in his dreams, he could not escape the horror his life had become.

21

JOHN WAS GETTING READY FOR Julian's wake when he heard the horn beep outside. It was raining so he jogged out to the minivan. Bruce was in the front seat and his mom was driving. Brett was in the back row of the minivan and barely acknowledged John as he entered. John had never seen Brett so upset before— he seemed like a different person.

When they arrived, John let out a long breath before entering the funeral home. He had only been to one wake when he was young and didn't remember much about it. He knew it was going to be an open casket and had already decided he would not look. He stood on line behind Bruce and Brett with sweaty palms. When they got closer, he saw the outline of Julian's figure in the coffin. *Wait, that's not Julian. It's just a body, inert and lifeless, just dead matter.*

John was next to go up to Julian's casket and his heart began to beat wildly. He watched Brett for signs of what to do. Brett said a prayer, crossed himself and then walked away. John would do the same. He walked towards the casket, his heart throbbing so horribly that he forgot to close his eyes. The sight was so awful he stared for a few seconds before he could shut them. The image stayed in his mind. As he knelt down, John trembled. *That's not Julian. It's just a body. But where is Julian?* He wanted the real Julian back, not the thing in the coffin. *Where did the real Julian go?*

Someone took hold of one of John's arms gently. He opened his eyes to see Bruce on one side and Bruce's mother on the other. Everyone stared as they helped him up and led him away from the coffin.

Bruce's mom held John for a long time in the hallway. "This will all be over soon, John," she kept saying, squeezing him hard.

On that gloomy day, the funeral hall was so packed with students, teachers, friends, family, and runners from all over that those who arrived late had to stand in the back. John had gotten there early with his mother and Shauna and found a seat very close to the front.

The funeral dragged by. Simon was asked to say a few words. John had to excuse himself for a little while. He just couldn't take it. He went to the bathroom and put some cold water on his face. Simon was almost done with his speech when he walked back in.

"But in our suffering we must remember, this was not an ordinary man. He was a man with big dreams. And it is up to us to carry on those dreams."

It had started to drizzle during the funeral procession and, by the time they reached the burial site, the rain had begun to come down heavily. John stared at the ground. It was sloped and little streams of water rolled by. A sick cry made his insides turn and he looked up. It was Julian's sister. He quickly turned his head back down. John tried to ignore the sobs and just wanted it to be over. He wanted to leave and get out right then and there.

A heavy arm fell on his shoulder and John looked over. It was Dower.

"Did you bring your gear?" Dower whispered.

John nodded.

"Good. You'll come in my car."

It was Tuesday, and like any other Tuesday, the runners were going to the Meadow.

After the burial, the rain began to taper off as they headed towards the Meadow. A tiny patch of sky opened at the horizon with tender blue light seeping through. John waited for a speech from Dower, but Dower just let the radio play and made small talk about the upcoming season. By the time they arrived, John thought he'd finally figured it out: There was just nothing to say. Dower wouldn't bring himself to utter common phrases like, *"Everything will be fine."* or *"He's in a much better place now."* He would not trivialize the moment. His response was silence, and it was the only response that preserved the sacredness of the things that could not be said.

When the runners were dressed and ready, Gary started them off at a good pace. The group was very quiet. The only noise that could be heard was the sneakers as they sloshed through the mud.

John didn't feel anything as he ran. The first time they went up the huge Cardiac Hill, his breathing changed, but he felt no pain. His body was numb and he didn't know whether he was running fast or slow. He was simply a machine doing work.

Then something strange happened at the summit of Cardiac Hill on the second loop: Gary stopped running.

"Stop!" Gary shouted at the others.

Those who had already started their descent had to come back up.

"What's going on?" one of the Milers asked.

Gary gave the man a hard look that silenced the Miler. Then he reached down into his sock and pulled out two things: The first looked like a playing card and the second a nail. John turned to Doc for a clue, but Doc simply shrugged.

"Let's have a moment of silence," Gary suggested.

Gary bowed his head and the other runners followed his lead.

Then he reached down and grabbed a huge rock lying on the side of the trail. Gary placed the card against the tree, set the nail, and hammered it in with three giant smashes. When he stepped away, John saw what the card was: Julian's epitaph.

"He will be there when each of you needs him the most," Gary said, nodding intensely at John and his teammates.

"Andiamos, men!" Gary said firmly as he started down the back of the hill.

John and some of the others hesitated a moment, awed by Gary's display of compassion.

When the runners exited the brush, they saw that a huge patch of sky had opened and bright rays of sunlight exploded through the hole. They passed Dower. He had not moved an inch, his blue eyes glaring out from under his umbrella, steady as a mountain.

On the final loop, the group tore across the course like caged animals set free. They stormed up Cardiac like it was a tiny bump. Everyone stayed with the main group, finishing hard together.

Brett and Alex fell to the ground as soon as they were done and John bent over, gasping heavily. Doc, Gary and the other Milers simply walked it off.

Gary looked at his watch and motioned Doc over. Doc looked at the watch and casually said, "It didn't feel that fast."

Dower went over to give the men some water, and Gary showed him the watch. "Faster than I've run here in years, Coach."

Dower nodded, not overly excited or surprised.

"We stopped for a moment too," Gary added.

In the meantime, the sky had filled with various hues of red and pink. The puddles in the parking lot looked like silver shadows, reflecting subtle hints of color from the sky. The landscape didn't seem like the Meadow anymore. It looked like a masterpiece by a great artist, a place that was far away, a place where everything was fine and perfect.

22

IT WAS JULIAN'S FRESHMAN YEAR, early fall, before the leaves had turned. The day was gray and cold with a light drizzle. After the freshman race, Dower had instructed Julian and the other freshmen to cool down for fifteen minutes, then cheer for the varsity team.

Everyone was making small talk when the first maroon jersey exploded from the brush. The Atlantic voices rose like a chorus. Three more maroon jerseys soon emerged. Two other runners passed, then the fifth maroon jersey. The crowd exploded again. Julian couldn't believe it. They had won a race with almost three hundred competitors by putting their team in the first seven places. It was nearly perfect.

Still, Julian had not a clue what he was in for. He did not yet know that Cardiac Hill lurked on the back of that course. It was the supreme judge of runners—so steep and long it would break runners and make them give up.

It was love at first sight. There was nothing more delightful than passing runners on that hill or watching them walk up it. At first, Julian would pass seven, eight, nine—sometimes more than ten—runners on the hill until he started leading races.

Julian loved that hill; he loved it like a woman. He would rush towards it as soon as he saw it. Once he hit the sharp incline, he would lean in with all his weight, driving up the steep surface with great determination until he reached the peak. There, on the brief plateau, came a dizzying silence. Then the great heart palpitations set in, his veins and arteries pumping at maximum capacity. Julian descended, feeling weightless, as if gravity were taking him. His stride would lengthen again and he would hit the level ground at a fast pace. Then he would become centered again, and continue driving through the back woods.

That great hill had never made Julian Seraphine walk or give up. The hill was his God and, on that sacred ground, he made a vow to dedicate his life to running.

23

SEVERAL NIGHTS LATER, MANY OF Julian's friends arranged a vigil on the track. John and Shauna arrived late and were surprised to find nearly 300 people on the track holding candles. A podium and a microphone were set up.

Maria, Julian's ex-girlfriend was reading a poem, "The flower that never bloomed, tomorrow's child, a star above."

Next, Bruce said he would read a poem that Brett had written. "It's called 'The Last Race.'"

Then suddenly, Brett snatched the poem from Bruce. "I'll read it." He cleared his throat and read:

Julian was born to race
Winning most of them
But there was one opponent
He couldn't outrun
Julian was never a quitter, though
He's still racing
On another course.

"I didn't know he had it in him," Shauna whispered.

"Me either," John replied.

The closing prayers soon came and each of the candles went its separate way.

John and Shauna decided they would go to the beach. John made her stop at the local convenience store first so he could get some beer. He grabbed a twelve-pack and brought it to the counter.

Atlantic five-year graduate Jerry Geofsky was working. "Where's the party tonight, Johnny boy?"

"Not sure," John said meekly, handing him the money.

"Where's Julian, bro? You guys always come in together."

"He's not coming out tonight." John snatched the bag and quickly walked out.

John and Shauna sat on the cool beach sand. John put down beer after beer as Shauna tried to make conversation. The sky was clear and the moon illuminated the ocean. Little waves crashed at the water's edge. Each one swelled, crested, and then broke, shooting a thin blanket of water towards them. The smooth pane then receded, falling back into the greater part from which it came. John thought about Julian's body from the wake the other day. *Just a body. But what about all the strength and power that once inhabited that body? Where could it have gone? It can't just be gone.*

Finally, he spoke, "What do you think happens when you die?"

Shauna was half-Jewish and half-Catholic—and unprepared for his question at best. "You go to heaven," she replied matter-of-factly.

John glared at her. "Heaven? You really believe that?"

"Yes, I do."

"That's such bull."

"Why? Julian believed it."

"No he didn't."

"He went to church all the time."

"He went to church to make his mom happy, Shauna."

"How do you know he didn't believe in it?"

John became agitated. "Because it's a fairy tale they tell you to make you feel good when someone dies."

"Well, I disagree."

John abruptly stood up.

"Oh come on, Shauna! He's in heaven now and everything's OK?"

Shauna looked up at him nervously. "Sit down, John."

"What about everyone still left here on earth? What about his family, his friends? What about me, Shauna?"

Shauna looked away.

John walked towards the water. "This was supposed to be our year."

Shauna stood up and walked close, then took his hand and made him sit back down with her. John finished three more beers before she suggested they leave.

They walked back towards the parking lot. When they reached the 6-foot stone wall that separated the sand from the street, John stopped. He walked back out on the sand and pointed to the stars. "Look, Shauna...there he is...a star above."

"Come on, John. Let's just go home."

He then took the bottle he was holding and threw it against the wall. The bottle shattered instantly. Shauna covered her head.

"Why?" John yelled into the sky. "Why?"

"Let's just go," Shauna cried.

Screw you! Screw you, God!" John shouted towards the sky as he collapsed to his knees. Shauna ran over and grabbed him, and he fell backwards on top of her. John started sobbing as she held him. She was crying, too, but held him until he stopped.

On the car ride home, neither of them spoke a word.

24

THE WORLD HAD BECOME GREY to John. Sunsets had lost their appeal, there was no escape from the thoughts and memories of the past and everything that used to be fun was gone, ruined and lost.

John was monk-like in his routine. He did not talk to anyone. Shauna kept calling, but John didn't pick up or return her messages. In silence, he washed dishes and cleaned and did his other work at the deli.

John ran each night and a few mornings as well, but runs were not blissful anymore. They seemed more like a chore to be done each day. He ran hard and fast, taking out his anger on his body. But no matter how hard he pushed himself, it brought him no pleasure.

Since camp was over, Simon had started to run in the mornings. He would put on his headphones and run far. He did the same route every day. Sometimes, he would also put in an extra few miles in the afternoon.

In the two weeks that followed, Brett ran more consecutive days than he had ever done on his own. Bruce started almost all of the runs with him, then after a few miles, Brett took off and Bruce stayed behind to time him.

Lowell and Alex still ran together every day. Lowell took the death better than Alex, who cried a lot. Benji occasionally ran with them.

Pedro handled it the best out of all of them. He wasn't new to death, and wasn't the kind of person to sit around and mourn. Pedro didn't change his routine much, he continued to work hard and run little.

That night, after his run, John lay on his bed, sipping a beer he brought home from the deli and listening to his Pearl Jam CD: *And now my bitter hands cradle broken glass of what was everything.*

25

A FEW NIGHTS LATER, JOHN decided to stop by Shauna's while he was on a run. They had not seen or spoken to each other since the night at the beach. The door opened and there she was, wearing a pair of shorts and tank top.

"I was just thinking about you," she said, hugging and kissing him.

"Hey," he responded dully.

She took his arm. "Come in."

"Can't."

"Why not?"

"I'm on a run. I just wanted to say hi."

"Come on, my parents are out…and won't be home for at least an hour or two."

John thought it over briefly.

"I'll drive you home later." She pulled hard this time and managed to move him off balance.

"I don't need you to drive me home," he muttered as he walked in.

As soon as they reached her room, they started kissing frantically. They fell onto the bed and soon their clothes made their way onto the carpet. Not long after, they were lying alongside each other in a much more relaxed state.

It was then a huge wave of guilt came over John. It was the first time that summer he had cut a run short. He got up and started to put his clothes on.

Shauna looked at him. "Don't worry, they'll be gone for another hour."

"I gotta go, Shauna."

"Not yet," she said, grabbing his shorts playfully.

"Give me them," John said, not joking.

After he dressed, he walked out of the room. Shauna followed him towards the front door. She just stared at him as he walked out.

John turned around on the steps and said, "I'm sorry." He shut the door behind him.

Just then, Shauna's parents' Jeep pulled up. John waved at them, thinking, *Some hour.*

He took out his pain and frustration on his body, increasing his pace as he continued his run. John was furious. He made repentance to Julian and swore he would never betray him again. Never again would he interrupt a run for a girl.

26

JOHN LOOKED OVER THE MEADOW as he executed a good quadriceps stretch. It was the last time they would meet there that summer and he was glad about that. Dower came over with a new runner.

"Boys, I want you to meet someone." He paused with furrowed brows. "Where's Pedro?"

Simon looked like he was about to say something but stopped himself.

"Spit it out, Simon," Dower said.

"I called his house."

"And?"

"His sister said he was out...with a girl."

"A girl?" Dower asked as if he had never heard of such a thing. He shook his head, and then nodded towards the new guy beside him. "Boys, this is Jack Irons. He won two state championships. He was also fourth at nationals."

Jack was built like a sprinter and his presence was intimidating. He had a short frame packed with more muscle than most distance runners, and also had thick, stubby thighs and calves the size of grapefruits.

Jack was a legend at Atlantic, running on the same team as

Doc. Though they were complete opposites, the two were best friends. He was always second to Doc, but was able to out-sprint him in some of the shorter races.

There were many stories about Jack. The stories were not of his great running feats but of his crazy behavior—checking runners in the back woods so hard that they fell down. One was knocked out after he hit a tree head-on. Off the track he was fearless, intimidating other teams, and a master at introducing the Atlantic team to any girls' team that might be at a meet or hotel.

"I'm sorry about your loss," Jack told them.

"Running again, Jack?" one of the Miler's called out.

"Just one loop," he replied.

John ran the three loops pretty much in silence. He, Simon and Brett kept up with the Miler's while most of the others fell back.

Doc had driven John, Alex and Lowell to the meadow. Jack Irons decided to go home in Doc's car, too.

After hearing so many crazy stories about Jack, John found him to be reserved. Jack only made small talk with Doc on the way home.

Then Alex asked, "Hey, Jack, what was your fastest high school mile time?"

"I ran a 4:09 mile my senior year in high school. Outdoors."

"What about college?"

"That was my best. I started getting a lot of knee pain my freshman year of college. I put the surgery off. It felt horrible, but I couldn't face going to the doctors. I guess I didn't want to know. I finally had the surgery the summer after my sophomore year, but it wasn't successful. I could barely walk for six months and the doctors told me to forget running at the college level."

The guys listened curiously.

"Over the next five years I had two more operations and the doctors told me to forget about running altogether. But that was five years ago." Jack paused and smirked. "But as you saw, I ran five miles tonight."

"Does it hurt now?" Lowell asked.

John elbowed Lowell.

"Sure, there's still pain, but it's nothing compared to the pain of not running."

Silence reigned until Doc dropped them off.

Jack turned to the boys. "You guys can do this. Just keep training hard and remember to be tough when it counts."

The boys nodded, and shook his hand as they exited the car.

27

JOHN TRIED TO RUN BUT the humidity in the air felt like a thick blanket covering his entire body. The weather was too gross to stay outside for a long period of time, but he couldn't stay inside anymore either. John had begun to feel like the walls were closing in on him.

That day his mom had planned a family barbeque for his Uncle Jimmy's birthday. The family had been there for close to an hour when John finally chose to leave his room and say hello.

"There he is," someone called as John walked in.

"Wow! Look how much he's grown!" one of his aunts exclaimed.

"He's almost as big as Jimmy."

"Hey, big guy," Uncle Jimmy said, putting an arm over John's shoulder. "Just about six feet now, huh?"

"What's with the long hair?" another uncle asked. "Protesting the war?"

"How's running going?" Jimmy asked.

"OK."

The questions kept coming and John started getting annoyed. "I gotta run out a second."

"Where?" one of his aunts asked.

"Ah…I forgot I have to help Shauna with something."

Jimmy grinned. "This one, always with the ladies."

John put on his running sneakers and took off. The sun was high in the sky, and John felt like he was running through a sauna. He started out fast, but with each stride, he seemed to lose more speed and energy. *Move faster!* he told himself. *Don't be weak!* But it was no use. The heat started to take its toll.

He ran a short loop and ended up on Julian's block. John hadn't been there since the night the team gathered there. He had not seen or spoken to Julian's family. When he saw that the door to Julian's house was open, he decided to stop.

John waited on the doorstep for a moment before pressing the doorbell. Julian's mother came to the door. There was nothing striking about her—she was an average women with dark hair, but John noticed she looked a lot older than he remembered her.

"Oh, hi, John," she said, surprised. She gave him a big hug. "Please come in."

She led him to the table. "Want some iced tea?"

"Sure."

She poured John a glass. It tasted as good as ever.

"How are you holding up?" she asked.

"I'm okay." There was a short moment of silence. "How…how have you been?" John asked, somewhat uneasily.

She poured more tea for him. "Oh, you know…I have my good days and my bad.

She looked at him intently. "You're still training hard everyday, right?"

He nodded.

They talked a little longer before she walked him out. At the door they embraced in a long hug again.

"Thanks so much for stopping by, John."

He looked back for a moment as he walked away and saw tears running down her cheeks.

John started off fast again. He felt refreshed, driven and inspired by the thought of Julian. He ran another three miles blindly through the heat and ended up at the cemetery.

It looked different than it had at the burial. Everything was alive—bright flowers all over—and the tombstones shining. It took him a little while to locate Julian's tombstone. John stared at the words, *"Beloved Son."* A peaceful silence came over him for the first time since Julian had passed on. And in that short moment, he was free of any thoughts, fears, and unrest within him. John forgot about all the noise, people, cars, businesses nearby. Then suddenly, the loud sound of a horn pulled him from his trance and back to reality.

John went to a party that night and drank a beer for himself, and then he drank one for Julian.

28

Julian was generally a happy, positive and inspirational person to the people around him. But dark forces threatened his existence. At times, feelings of doubt and worthlessness consumed him. There were times when he hated everyone and everything. He did not know or understand where the feeling had come from. How his mind worked scared him and, just when he thought it was safe, it deceived him.

Julian spent confusing late nights wondering what it was all about. The world seemed to have little or no meaning. He wondered, what was the point? Go to school, get a job, marry, buy a house, and that was it? A life defined by brand name stores and weekends? That could not be the meaning of life.

Julian believed people lived from a place of preconceptions and fixed notions about things they believed to be true. They were convinced about what was possible within themselves and in life before even attempting it, and they never challenged or questioned anything. They were convinced of all the things they could not do. But he knew the world was built largely on false notions.

Julian was convinced of the opposite. The dead, dreary hours when the mind was filled with doubt and confusion—the hours when one was lost and depressed, and starving for purpose—that was not the truth. It was just the result of a world running on false conclusions and people living fake lives.

When he was running, the truth came out. The deep inhalations, the slight breeze in his face—even the pain could be delightful in this context because it made him feel alive. It took Julian from the barren and dark world he resided in, and transported him to a new one—a destination ripe with possibility, a place that was so open and wide he seemed to melt into it.

Julian realized something from his direct experience with pain and suffering, from the day-in and day-out, backbreaking training. When he was completely exhausted and nearly fainting, one ultimate truth had arisen: Nothing in life was fixed.

Julian could explain little of this earth. At times, he didn't know who he was, what his place in the world was, or where he was headed. But when he was running, things always made sense. Julian needed to run like he needed to breathe. And it was only then, as he charged through the streets, that the demons settled down and the angels appeared.

29

JOHN WAS GETTING DRESSED WHEN the doorbell rang and peeked through the blinds to see who it was. When he saw Simon, a feeling of despair came over him.

"Wanna go for a run?" Simon asked.

"I can't. I have to go to work," John said coldly.

"Oh."

There was a long, awkward silence.

"Okay, well...I guess I'll see you at camp," Simon said.

John nodded. "Yeah, see you then."

John felt guilty as he shut the door, but he didn't know what to say. It just wasn't the same between them anymore—not just him and Simon—but any of the guys.

John didn't run that next day. It was the first day he had taken off since he had started in June. That night, as he packed for camp, Shauna called and asked if she could come over to say goodbye. John wasn't in a good mood, but told her she was welcome.

John was stuffing things into his duffel bag when Shauna arrived. She objected to his manner of packing and began taking his clothes out, folding them, then putting them back in. It was a nice gesture, but everything she did or said managed to irritate him. He barely said a word to her and she eventually ended up talking to John's mom in the other room.

Later on, John got a call from Brett, who invited him to go to a party. He asked Shauna if she wanted to go and she said okay. On the way, he asked her to stop at 7-Eleven so he could get beer. She accepted, but only after a long fight. Shauna told John he needed to calm down with his drinking.

"Oh, be quiet!" John told her and walked off.

Shauna followed him into the party but he didn't really want to be around her. He did his best to ignore her, and finally she took the hint. She made sure to curse him out before she walked out.

"What's that all about?" Brett asked with a grin.

"Don't worry about it," John said.

John didn't have much fun at the party. He sat mostly in silence, drinking. The kid who was hosting the party kicked everyone out of his house early. John and Brett ended up sitting on the bleachers until late.

"I miss him," Brett said.

It caught John off guard and he simply nodded.

"Do you think we can do it without him?"

John paused again. "I don't know."

They sat in silence for a while.

John asked, "So what's this camp like?"

"It's wonderful. All the guys shower together every night."

"Seriously, retard."

"No parents and girls in bikinis all day by the lake. You might have to do a few runs, but, overall, it's paradise."

John shook his head. "You are so full of it."

"You'll see, Johnny Boy, you'll see."

30

MOST OF THE TEAM WAS already at the school when John arrived.

Dower was busy interrogating Pedro. "Where were you Tuesday?"

"I told you, Coach. I had to work with my dad."

Dower knew he was lying, but didn't press the issue. Instead, he turned towards the others. "Everyone say goodbye to your parents. We'll be leaving in five minutes."

As the kids entered the bus, Dower took a head count. Someone was missing. "Where is Brett?" he shouted.

No one answered.

"I don't care, this time we're not waiting for him," Dower said.

As the bus pulled away, a car sped into the parking lot. Bruce honked a few times and waved at Dower as Brett jumped out and ran toward the bus. He was barefoot, wearing a white t-shirt and boxer shorts, and carrying a large garbage bag.

Dower stopped him before he could sit down.

"What the heck is the matter with you? Do you know how much glass is in that parking lot? Where are your sneakers?" Dower asked.

"In my bag." Brett held up the garbage bag.

"Go sit down," Dower said, shaking his head.

As Brett walked through the bus, the girls made quite a stir about his outfit. Brett hiked up his boxer shorts a little and the girls went crazy, trying to pull them down.

"Oh, stop that, Mary!" Brett shouted in a high pitched voice.

"SIT DOWN, O'CONNER!" Dower boomed.

John was tired, and fell asleep soon after the bus pulled off. When he woke up, they were far from Long Island. The landscape had changed, almost all traces of development had vanished, and tan and green fields stretched towards the horizon.

Camp was in upstate New York, probably not far from where his dad now lived. After his parents divorced, he moved upstate to live with another woman—a woman his father had been seeing for a good while before the divorce, John imagined. He had visited there once, years ago, the summer after the divorce, and it was very uncomfortable for John. He resented his father, his new girlfriend and her small children. Ultimately, John left, hitchhiking to a local bus stop. His dad had called him a few times since then, but John never returned his calls.

He dozed off again until they arrived. The bus took a left down a shady, small road and stopped a half-mile in.

At first look, it seemed like an abandoned sleep-away camp, empty and closed up for the summer. A dozen redwood cabins were scattered over an acre of grass and were surrounded by large, leafy trees. John noticed a few tennis and basketball courts, but he didn't see a lake. Overall, he was unimpressed.

The bunks at the camp were assigned by ability, usually determined by the coaches. Dower also thought it was wise to split some of the varsity up so there was less of a chance they would misbehave. He put Pedro and Simon in Bunk one, Brett in two, Alex and John in three, Lowell four, and Benji was in seven.

Each day there were two runs—one in the morning and one in the afternoon. The morning run was always the longest since the weather was cooler then. Each bunk had to do the morning run together, but the afternoon runs could be done with any bunk as long as a counselor was notified.

The run on the first afternoon was a nice, easy run. John's bunk made their way along a small, shady road that bordered the camp. Soon, John was met with endless open fields and small mountains in the distance. There were a few old, rural farm houses with great distances between them. Some of them had old, broken down cars in the yard. John searched around, but didn't see any moving cars or people. The distant points were filled with colors he wasn't used to—hues of brown and yellow.

The blacktop of the roads and the lines painted on them seemed pristine, as if they had barely been used. John ran up and down the long, gradual hills and began to feel a sense of serenity. Part of him felt different. He knew he had never been to this place before, but deep down inside he felt he knew this place well, as if from some other time or some other life he had lived.

Afterwards, John went down by the lake with Alex. The body of water stretched between mountains and a field of grass acted as a beach. Astonished, John realized Brett wasn't lying—there were girls in swimsuits all over, lying on towels on the grass or jumping from the dock into the dark cold water. One girl was causing a commotion—a particularly overdeveloped girl, in a small American flag bikini. John kept hearing some of boys sing the star spangled banner, and for good reason.

Brett and Pedro had parked their stuff near a group of Baldwin girls they knew. One of the girls immediately caught John's eye. She was wearing a black bikini and lying on her side.

A kid came up to say hello to the Atlantic boys. "Hey, guys! Where's Julian?"

John walked down to the lake and jumped in. The water was very cold, but felt good against his skin and head, which had become hot. He stayed immersed in the cold water for some time before he got out. His towel was still by the others so he decided to sit on the deck and sun dry.

Soon, some of the others came down to swim. One of the

Baldwin girls, Amy, sat next to John and started asking him questions.

"So, John, do you have a girlfriend?" Amy asked.

"No," Brett answered for him.

Amy smiled towards her friend. "John, this is Leah." John turned around to see the girl in the black bikini standing behind him.

John introduced himself, and spent the rest of the afternoon talking and flirting with the girls.

31

LATER THAT NIGHT, JOHN LEARNED a huge lesson. Although the daytime temperature in upstate New York was hot, it dropped significantly at night. The light blanket he packed was no match and soon he was scrambling in the dark for his sweatshirt and sweatpants.

He was glad when the early sunlight came through his windows. At 7:30, the bugle called, and everyone rose and made their way into the bathroom. When John finished washing up, he noticed Alex was still in bed looking rather warm and cozy. John picked up one side of the bed and Alex rolled onto the floor.

"AGGHH! What the hell?"

"Time to get up!"

"Breakfast isn't mandatory," Alex said, getting back in his bed.

"Oh, sorry." John chuckled.

John soon realized that half the kids were not present. Those who did eat were advised to eat a light breakfast, because they only had about an hour and half to digest their food before the first of the day's two runs.

That morning, John's bunk went for a nice seven miler on the hills. Before the run, one of John's counselor's, Laird, laid out the rules for the bunk and the run. Laird was an ex-marine and championship sprinter in college. He spoke like a military commander. The kids kept staring at each other as he spoke, trying not to laugh. Their other counselor, Davey, was a championship college runner and one of Doc's teammates. They also had an older, head counselor, but he didn't say much.

The group was quiet, the boys feeling each other out. Most of the kids were from New York, but there were also kids from New Jersey and some of the other nearby states. A lot of the kids were not direct competitors for the Atlantic runners; they would only see each other at the big races.

A few miles into the run, a few boys started pushing the pace.

"Hey, get back here!" Laird shouted. "Do that again and you're going home."

At night, the kids hung out by the canteen. John spotted Leah immediately. She was wearing jeans and a red, hooded sweatshirt. Her brown hair fell into the hood in waves.

Several guys were trying to talk to Leah, including John's teammates, so he decided to play it cool. He took a walk around the canteen and found Doc speaking with the large group of kids on the other side.

"At any moment in a race, a runner has a choice. He can either give in to the pain or transcend it. At each moment, there is an opportunity to turn things around. As each runner passes you there is an opportunity to go with them."

"Because this fact is true: No race in life is ever fixed," Doc said.

Later in the night, Leah came over to John to talk. They made small talk. She seemed very interested in him and asked a lot of questions. John found her quite beautiful and sweet, and though he wasn't in the best mood, he didn't mind answering her questions.

32

ATLANTIC HAD ALWAYS BEEN THE outlaws of the local track and field circuit. Though the team had lost some of its reputation on the track, it hadn't off the track. Brett was the biggest and most-feared, but he was also the most-popular kid in camp. Pedro was an instigator and had Brett to back him up. The Atlantic guys were also good friends with some of the Baldwin guys, particularly Willy and Todd.

Brett's bunk became the big hangout and they had a walk-by-at-your-own-risk policy. Water balloons were shot out at high speeds, and water guns took aim at all girls—especially ones in white t-shirts.

The team was sitting in front of Brett's bunk when a small vehicle approached them. Upon closer inspection, they saw Dower in the driver's seat of a golf cart. Dower was in pretty good shape so it seemed more of a luxury than a necessity. Lowell was sitting beside him wearing a brand-new white hat that hadn't been broken in yet.

"Hot ride," Brett joked.

"You guys having fun?" Dower asked.

The team nodded.

"You can get off now, Lowell," Dower demanded.

Lowell grabbed his bag and jumped off the golf cart. Pedro whispered something in Brett's ear as Dower drove away and Brett nodded.

"Hey guys—" Lowell started to say after sticking out his hand. But before he could finish his comment, Brett had him over his shoulders.

Flushing was an Atlantic ritual. The ritual consisted of dunking a freshman's head in a toilet bowl (or in Lowell's case, a junior). The initiate had a choice: he could either dunk his head in himself or, if he resisted, it would be done for him. Some put up a fight, but most freshmen volunteered. Brett was the best example of resistance. He took on four seniors during his initiation. It was bloody, and while his head was split open in the process, his hair remained dry.

Julian had never been flushed and found it vulgar to participate in such events. He took a walk while the action was happening.

A crowd had already gathered in Brett's bunk near the bathroom area.

"What's going on here?" one of Brett's counselors shouted as he pushed through the crowd.

Brett and Pedro froze, and the room fell silent.

"Freshman initiation," Brett answered.

The counselor hesitated and said, "I wasn't here." Then he walked out.

The crowd cheered and patted him on the back as he exited. Brett flipped Lowell like a pancake while Pedro flushed him. Lowell finally came up gasping for air. When he walked out, his shirt was soaked.

Pedro came out with Lowell's white hat and handed it to him. "No hard feelings, right?" Pedro flashed a devilish smile.

Lowell accepted the hat. But when he placed it on his head, a huge cloud of white smoke filled the air around him. Everyone laughed. Pedro had filled it with Gold Bond powder. Annoyed, Lowell left.

Then Brett pointed to Benji and jokingly shouted, "Let's get the freshman!"

Benji took off faster than a rabbit and they all burst with laughter.

When Brett and Pedro and the others made their way down to the lake, they were surprised at what they saw. The beautiful girl in the red, white and blue bikini was helping Lowell wash his hair by the lake.

While training was the focus during the day, motivation was the focus in the evening. At night, the kids gathered in a large gymnasium or on the outside stage to listen to one of the counselors—most elite college runners—or a guest speaker.

Doc was one of the speakers that evening. He received a loud round of applause and paced a little before beginning his speech. "My senior year of high school at the indoor nationals we were running the 4 x 800. It was snowing out and had been all day. The team hadn't lost a race all season and we had the best time in the country. There was only one team in the race who was close—Brookstone—and their anchor leg had won the individual 800 the day before.

I was the anchor and received the baton in first place with a three second lead. I had the race in the bag, with one lap to go. On this last lap, Brookstone's anchor caught me. Their anchor and I ran head-to-head until the last 30 yards, where he beat me by two-tenths of a second and set a new national indoor record.

All I remember is the black uniform shooting past me. It was the most devastating loss of my life. It was the first time I had given everything I had and lost. The Brookstone team and everyone watching went nuts at the upset and no one on our team could believe it.

I was incredibly upset. I just wanted to be alone so after the race, I jogged outside. There was snow all over. I looked at the silver medal, a symbol of my being second in the nation and threw it as far as I could." Doc paused. "I stayed outside for a while, afraid to face my coach and teammates.

Finally, my best friend came out to get me. He said it was the greatest race he'd ever seen. I said, 'Yeah, but we lost.' 'Both teams broke the national record and you ran a personal best,' he said. 'What more can you ask for?' 'The gold,' I replied.

He just looked at me for a moment, then said, 'We all did, Jimmy, we all did.' Then he went back in and left me outside." Doc's face turned serious. "It took me a while to get over that loss, but I learned a huge lesson that night. That one race didn't make me any less of a runner. In fact, that race was the most important race of my life because I could have given up. I could have said, 'I will never be the best in this sport. There will always be someone better and never given it my all again.'" Doc paused again. "But this sport is not about gold or glory. It's about not giving up when it gets tough."

There was a huge round of applause.

"Thanks guys, and good luck in the upcoming season," Doc concluded.

Dower came over to the team afterwards and asked, "Did you boys enjoy the speeches?"

"Amazing!" Benji answered, still beaming.

"I want to race right now!" Alex exclaimed.

Lowell had remained silent the entire time. Dower turned to him. "Lowell, any brain activity at all going on up there?"

"He was…great. I loved…I loved the part where the guy said it was the only thing he was ever good at."

Dower nodded and gave Lowell a hard pat on the shoulder. "Behave tonight, boys."

33

On the fourth day, John opened up. The claustrophobia that he had been feeling at home released. Each run was like a meditation that cleansed his soul. His problems dissolved into the open scenery of the mountains. John felt better about his situation and Julian's death.

He wondered about the kind of training he could do if he lived in such an area. He felt if he did live there he would not use a watch, he would just run until he got tired, or it became dark out.

There was so little development compared to Long Island. It seemed a simpler life. He imagined the people cared less about style and fashion here. It didn't seem a bad way to live.

A simpler life, that is what he craved.

Long Island was a place of rampant materialism. Status seemed to be defined by cars, clothes and the town one lived in. Even in Atlantic— a blue collar town—it was easy to get caught up in it. School could be a popularity contest, and often, Julian simply wanted nothing to do with it. Sure, he was a popular and well-liked individual. But he knew there was more to life, more than having a hot girlfriend, getting good grades and applying to the best colleges.

The other kids seemed to be content with the status quo. For him, going out and partying, going after girls, and goofing around was simply not enough. He always felt like there was something missing, something that was not found in his textbooks or on TV.

When Julian came to Atlantic, found Dower, Doc, and the Milers, he knew he had found what he was always looking for. They were the real deal. There was nothing fake about any of them, and they could not be taken away from their passion for running.

Many kids felt a need to be different by changing their appearance. But Julian did not need to get piercings or to color his hair or take steroids. He did not need to dress or look a certain way. To be a runner was not to look a certain way. Running was not a sport. It was a lifestyle. If he did not compete, his life had no meaning.

Julian did not like to speak about running with people who did not understand it. He did not like to discuss it with his family and friends who did not run.

Furthermore, he did not like the idea of people running to keep in shape. Julian did not consider running exercise. He did not do it to keep in shape nor did any of his teammates. These poor people, Julian thought, stuck in some fantasy their society had created for them and striving for an American ideal—a skinny waist and tight ass, chiseled abs and a sculpted torso. For them, the most important thing in the world was to be thin and to look like an advertisement. And Julian ran in protest of those ideals.

The running that those people did had nothing to do with the running Julian and the Milers did. There was no Lycra or running technology embedded into the fabric of their clothing. He and the Milers still used cotton and most had mid-grade sneakers, at best. Water and sweat-proof clothing made no sense to them. That's what they were there for—to be drenched with water or sweat, and their shoes were meant to get heavy with water or mud. None of them were interested in body fat nor the shape of their thighs, calves and waist.

Even the concept of a runner's high was amusing to him. Sure, *there were times when Julian experienced a high during or after training. But it was only a small part of an overall grueling experience. And what about the runner's low? No one dare talk about the times when a runner doubted himself and his own abilities; the times when he believed he would not finish a workout or race. The times when the runner was simply overwhelmed with pain and doubt. When his conscious mind told him to stop, to slow and give up—that the task he wanted to achieve was simply impossible for the human body he inhabited. These instances required the truest test of his heart. Yet, these moments were rarely, if ever, discussed.*

Running was not something to be taken lightly. That was not why runners chose the lifestyle. It was not their religion either; it did more for them than their old religion ever could. There was no speculation involved, no stories, nor a life that had to be lived in fear and guilt. Running was a powerful act—something the body, mind and soul could immediately grasp and take part in.

And Julian knew once this commitment was made there were no limits to where running could take him. Running was like a drug and the destinations were unfathomable. One could go high and low, and as deep as the runner chose. But this drug would not kill him— no, each day, it only made him stronger.

34

BRETT AND JOHN WERE TOSSING a lacrosse ball back and forth when Dower's cart pulled up next to John. "Whose sticks are those?"

John thought about it a moment. "Brett's."

"I don't want to see them again."

"I'll tell him."

"Meeting at the bleachers tonight at seven," Dower informed. John nodded.

At dinner Benji brought up an interesting point. "Who is Irvington's fifth man?"

"It doesn't matter, we killed them in that race," Brett said with a mouth full of food.

"Yeah, but their whole team wasn't there," Alex responded.

"Yeah, but their whole team sucks," Pedro said.

"Patole is their fifth man," Simon informed them.

"Who?" Brett asked.

"Jim Patole, the freshman phenom. He's their fifth man and he wasn't at the race."

"That kid sucks," Pedro said and twisted his lip.

"Well, he ran 16:30 this summer in a road race," Simon said.

"Who told you that?" Pedro asked.

"Dower."

"Whatever," Pedro said. "He's fast on the road, but I'll kill him on the course."

"I'll flat out kill him," Brett shouted. Mashed potatoes flew out of his mouth and landed on Benji's shirt. The team had a good laugh while Benji frowned.

After dinner, the team had a meeting with Dower on the bleachers. The sun had just set and the sky was wild and furious with bold patterns of swirling color. The tranquil hiss of evening settled in.

Dower appeared suddenly from the darkness like a ghost. All laughing and joking stopped when he cleared his throat.

"I've been watching all of you train in the past few days and one thing has become apparent: You're all in the best shape of your life." He paused a brief moment. "The thing is…I don't know whether it's enough."

There was a low stir within the group.

"Right now, on paper, every team here has seven runners of equal or better caliber. But Simon is coming back from serious injuries. Brett has been inconsistent at best all year. Lowell and John have made remarkable improvements, but they're going up against tough, seasoned runners. Benji's talent looks promising, but he lacks experience. Lastly, our team doesn't have much depth and, if someone gets hurt, we will be in serious trouble."

Dower paused again. "Now, I know what each of you is asking yourselves right now: After everything he just said, how are we going to do this? Well, the answer is quite simple: The same way we've always done it. We will outwork every other team." He paused again before raising his voice, "I'm going to say it again: We are going to outwork every team.

Yes, we've experienced a tragedy, but that tragedy has brought us closer, and our purpose is stronger than it's ever been." He quieted to let the thought sink in. "I know there's a lot of pressure on all of you already, but I want you to know it's only going to get tougher. But you must remember something, when things do get tough this season. You are not just running for yourself."

Dower straightened up and concluded, "Okay, well, have fun at the dance tonight and remember: No means no."

Silence followed Dower's departure until Pedro spoke. "Come on, let's go. We're gonna be late."

Everyone ran to their bunks to get ready, except John and Simon, who walked back slowly.

"You think we can really do this, Simon?"

"We don't have a choice, John."

John nodded, while taking a deep breath of air into his lungs.

Alex was nearly dressed, fixing his hair and dosing himself with cologne, when John got back to the bunk. John lay down on his bed. "Easy on the cologne, little man."

"What are you doing?" Alex asked, somewhat exasperated that John wasn't dressed. "I'm not waiting for you."

"I don't think I'm going."

"What? You're crazy!" Alex said as he sped out of the bunk.

John stayed behind while, one by one, the other kids left, and he put on his Discman. The deep, resonant moans of the singer seemed to perfectly mimic the emotions he felt deep within his body: *"I wait up in the dark/ for you to speak to me."*

John thought about what Dower had said. It was the first time he had expressed doubt since Julian passed away. And there was a lot of truth in what he had said. On paper, their team was nothing. They barely had five guys. Was it really possible that they could win the county and state title? Or was the entire thing just a fantasy Julian had dreamed up? As John lay there, listening to the music, no answers came.

"If he's in there, he's definitely playing with himself," Willy said as the crew approached John's bunk.

"There he is!" Brett said, jumping on John. Then he started humping him.

"Get off me!" John said, struggling to push Brett's big frame off.

"You're going like that?" Pedro asked.

"I'm not going," John snapped.

"I think I can change your mind," Willy said, reaching into his backpack to brandish a bottle of whisky.

"Where did you get that?"

"Brought it from home," Willy replied.

"By the way, that hot girl likes you," Brett told John.

"What?"

"You heard what I said. Now get dressed."

The woods behind the bunks extended for over a mile. The boys sat around talking and sipping whiskey. Brett made a small camp fire.

"Long summer," Willy finally said, putting a hand on Simon's shoulder and breaking the silence.

Simon nodded.

"So you guys have a real shot at winning or what?" Todd asked.

"We're gonna destroy you guys," Pedro said.

"Especially with our secret weapon," Brett said.

"Who's that?" Willy asked.

"Him." Brett pointed to John.

Willy looked at John. "Oh yeah? You gonna win counties?"

"Counties? He's gonna win the state meet," Pedro said.

"State meet?" Willy asked with a wry face.

It was silent again for awhile. Then, out of nowhere, John started laughing and everyone stared at him.

"What's so funny?" Brett asked.

"Remember the time…remember when Julian ripped the fire alarm off the wall?"

Pedro and Brett started laughing.

"Wait! Fire alarm? What are you talking about?" Simon asked.

Brett whispered something to Todd and Willy and they both started laughing.

"So *Julian* did that?" Simon shouted. "I got grounded for three weeks and had to pay my dad thirty-five dollars because of that!"

John was laughing so hard he fell over and Brett soon joined him. He rolled so fast that he almost landed in the fire, making them all laugh even harder.

"Jerk!" Simon said as he looked up towards the heavens, shaking his head. Then he smiled and began laughing with the others.

"We should get goin'," Willy said.

A dance floor had been set up on the basketball court. John didn't feel like dancing so he sat on a nearby hillside. He watched as his friends rubbed themselves against every female they could. Brett and Todd even danced with the female counselors, who probably didn't realize they were campers.

John lay back and looked up at the sky. It was much different than where he lived. The stars looked like giant jewels instead of small, dismal lights.

He noticed a small figure standing near him.

"How come you're not dancing?" a girl asked.

John sat up, somewhat startled. The he saw Leah's beautiful face. She was dressed nice and looked rather breathtaking, he thought.

"Not in the mood. What about you?"

"Not in the mood to have guys rubbing up on me."

"You mean my teammates?"

She chuckled.

"Want to take a walk?" he asked, standing up.

"Okay," she said.

He took her hand. It was small and slightly cool to the touch. They walked down by the lake where they found a bench to sit on. The lake was perfectly still, lit by the stars and moon.

"I'm sorry about your teammate," Leah said.

"Oh, it's okay," John said quietly and looked away.

She seemed to hesitate before continuing. "I met him here last summer. He seemed like a really great guy."

"He was."

This time she took his hand. He gave her a little smile. The gesture suddenly made John feel comfortable. His emotional dam spilled. He told Leah about his entire summer with Julian. Things he had never told anyone. John spoke for a long time and she listened intently.

"He was so different than everyone else," John said. "He wasn't the fastest guy I ever raced, but he was so tough…he just wouldn't give up. That's why he was so great at cross country. He would have won the state title, I know he would have."

As John locked onto her gaze, a tear fell from Leah's right eye. Then there was a long silence during which Leah wiped her eyes. John waited for her to look back towards him, and when she did, he leaned in slowly. Her lips were soft to the touch. They kissed slowly between breaths.

Suddenly, a bright light shined upon them and a stern voice said, "Curfew, folks!"

Leah gasped and pulled away.

"I'll give you five seconds to say goodnight," the voice said as the flashlight turned off.

Leah gave him a quick kiss on the cheek and said, "I'll see you tomorrow, John." Then she scurried off.

"Yeah, tomorrow," John mumbled, holding in his anger.

The figure moved towards him. "John?"

John then realized it was Doc.

"Hey buddy, how's it going?" Doc asked.

"Could be a lot better."

"There's always tomorrow, stud."

"Yeah, right." John twisted his lip.

When John reached the bunk, he noticed Alex was not back yet. Later on, after the lights were out, a figure woke him up, shaking him repeatedly.

"John? John! I made out with Amy!" Alex whispered excitedly.

John murmured, "Good." Then he rolled over and put his head under his blanket.

35

JOHN WOKE UP EARLY THE next morning. His head ached and an intense thirst plagued him. He could not fall back asleep so he walked to the dining area.

The sun had just risen. The field was still wet with dew. The juice machine was out of everything except cranberry, and even that tasted watery, so he decided to just drink water.

The sun started to come over the bunks and warmed him as he walked back to the bunk. The Bugle sounded. Hopefully, he would be able to fall back asleep, and planned on skipping the morning run.

"Early start?" The familiar voice called as John reached the bunk.

John turned around, horrified to see Dower on his golf cart.

"Yeah...I was thirsty."

"You guys are going to run in pairs this morning. You're running with Brett. Go tell him while I pair up the others," Dower requested. "We'll have a short meeting after breakfast by the bleachers."

So much for skipping the morning run, he thought.

When John entered Brett's bunk, he immediately noticed

something strange. No one had responded to the wake up call. And apparently, Brett wasn't the only one not doing the morning run.

"Brett, wake up."

Brett didn't budge.

"Brett, *wake up!*" John insisted.

Again, no response. John ripped off his covers.

Brett moaned, barely moving. "What do you want?"

"Get up. You have to run today."

"What are you talking about?"

"Coach is pairing us up and we also have a meeting."

"Aw, this sucks!" Brett said as he sat up.

"It's not gonna be that bad. Everyone's going to the Woodstock site today. It's just three and a half miles away."

"SSShhhh!" Brett's counselor demanded.

John stared at him in disbelief.

They decided to run with John's bunk since they really had no other choice. The group was scheduled to run to the site of the original Woodstock and it was supposed to be an easy run. They would stop for water at the site and have some time to look around.

A headache and nausea set in a mile into the run. Neither John nor Brett said a word. When they arrived some of the bunks were already there. John drank some water and walked around. It wasn't very exciting. There was an engraved stone that served as a memorial and a UV filled with a couple of hippies that looked like they had never left the original gathering.

"Let's get out of here," Brett said.

John nodded.

About a half-mile from the site, John heard someone shouting at them. John turned to see Laird, one of his counselors.

"Brett, hold up," John said. "I think he's telling us to come back."

"So? Let him catch up and tell us."

The shouting kept getting louder, and soon they could hear Laird's rapid strides. He broke between them, grabbing each of them hard by the arm. "What are you two, deaf?" he shouted.

"Don't get your panties in a bunch. We know how to get back and—"

Before Brett could finish the sentence, Laird swept him and secured a lock on him.

"Aaagghhh!" Brett groaned.

John moved in, but Laird was a trained fighter and saw it coming.

"John, stay back or you *will* be hurt!" Laird warned.

"Get him off me!" Brett shouted.

John looked around for help and saw someone coming towards them. It was his other counselor, Davey.

"Tell him to get off!" John shouted.

"What's going on, Laird?" Davey asked as he came close.

Laird didn't respond.

"Come on, Laird, that's enough," Davey insisted.

Laird stared at him for a moment before letting him go. Brett sprung off the ground.

"Just a little discipline lesson, that's all," Laird reasoned.

"Psycho!" Brett shouted.

"You okay?" Davey asked Brett.

Just then, the rest of group approached. The head counselor was an older, graying gentleman and asked, "Everything all right, boys?"

"We're fine," Laird answered.

"Great, then let's head back."

"I'll take the two Atlantic boys back," Laird said.

The head counselor gave him a curious look.

"They want to run a little harder," Laird said.

"No, I think they're fine," Davey interjected.

"Okay, you both go with them," the head counselor said as he led the other group off.

Laird grinned. "So you boys want to run, huh? Then we'll run."

"Let's do it!" Brett shouted.

John rolled his eyes and cursed Brett silently.

Laird started them off at a good pace. Brett was on Laird's right, and John and Davey trailed behind them. Soon, the group caught up to the bunk and passed them.

Two miles later, the hot sun beat down on John's head and shoulders. He was thirsty and tired. The pace was still fast, but at least they were close to camp.

"How you guys feeling?" Laird asked sarcastically.

"Great," Brett shot back.

Laird chuckled. "Turn left at the crossroads."

"That's not the way back to camp," Davey pointed out.

"I know," Laird grinned widely.

John's face painfully contorted when he recognized which route Laird was taking them back on, Everest. Everest Street was Cardiac Hill's distant relative—except it was actually made up of three steep hills, each one as steep as Cardiac. John cursed Brett again.

Laird picked up the pace as the first hill came into sight. The two stayed head-to-head for most of the first incline. Then Brett broke ahead and ferociously charged upward.

Laird was a sprinter and caught Brett easily on the slight dip before the second incline started. But on the next climb, Brett moved ahead again. Laird was faster, but Brett was tougher, and his long legs made him an excellent hill climber

John and Davey had lost ground on the two, but started to catch Laird as he started to fatigue.

"Let's bury this guy," Davey told John.

On the middle of the second incline, they caught Laird. He was breathing heavily and moving slowly.

"Distance caught up to you, huh, Laird?" Davey asked. "Gotta respect the distance."

Laird didn't respond as they passed him.

On the third incline, Brett slowed a little and they were able to catch him. The three reached the summit in unison. Once they reached the top, they slowed down a bit.

Brett turned around, held up his favorite finger, and yelled, "See you back at camp, loser!"

It was only a mile and a half back to camp and the three took it slow. When they were done, Davey turned to them and said, "If you two keep up that mentality, you're going to be unstoppable this season."

Dower was standing near the main entrance when they walked in. "Everything all right, Davey?"

"Yes, Coach," Davey replied.

"You didn't come back with the group."

"We wanted to run a little extra," Brett interjected.

Dower studied him. "What happened to your face?"

There were scratches on Brett's face from when it had hit the black-top.

"I tripped…and fell down," he answered.

"Well, go get some lunch before it's over," Dower said calmly. "Davey, hang back a moment, will you?"

The two rushed toward the cafeteria and found the workers putting away the food as they entered. They grabbed what they could. John took as many drinks as would fit on the tray. Then they went out to eat on the grass.

As they were finishing, they heard Dower screaming from the main office. Not long after, Laird came out of the office red-faced. John and Brett exchanged looks and started laughing.

John slept the rest of the day, not rising until dinner. It was then that Alex delivered the bad news.

"Leah found out at about your girlfriend," he told John.

"How?"

"She's friends with some Irvington girls that are here."

"Great," he regretted.

36

THE LAST DAY OF CAMP was a sad scene. Though it was only a week, many kids made new friends—even some girlfriends.

John threw all his clothes into a duffle bag so it didn't take him long to pack. As he headed out, someone grabbed his arm. It was Davey.

"Good luck this season, Buddy. I'll be looking for your name in the papers," Davey told him.

John walked towards the buses. His teammates were gathered in front.

"No way!" Pedro shouted, pointing to Lowell, who was making out with the beautiful girl who had helped him clean his head earlier that week.

"Get on the bus!" Dower called.

As John left the fertile terrain of upstate New York, the reality of camp and summer ending began to set in. The fact that school was approaching and cross country was starting began to weigh down on his shoulders heavily. John felt as if he was drowning in a whirlwind of emotions.

If his relationship with Shauna was not dwindling away, it was certainly in serious jeopardy. And John also felt horrible about Leah. He wanted to talk to her, but he didn't know what to say. Besides, there were more important matters than girls to worry about. And no matter what happened, he knew running was to be his main focus.

The last day of camp always snuck up on Julian, as it did to most of the campers after the near-paradise week. Then the horrible realization set in—not only was camp over, but so was summer. The emotions would tear at Julian's heart, but like water slipping through his grasp, there was nothing he could do to stop it. No one could stop the seasons from changing. And while part of Julian clung tightly to the old, another part of him yearned for the new. Soon enough, he would forget his despair and become terribly excited about the fall. It was cross country season, and what would this season be if it did not parallel the miraculous changes that occurred in the land.

37

THERE WAS PRACTICE A FEW days before school began. A low-pressure system had moved into the region and the cool North breeze felt good as John jogged to school that morning. He always preferred to train in the cooler weather.

The first thing Dower did was announce that Simon was the captain and no one was surprised by the decision. Though Simon was not the best runner, he had the most dedication and certainly was the most mature.

Dower instructed them to run to Mill Pond. Mill Pond was a nature preserve located near the southern border of Atlantic. A black-top path spanned around the pond. The path was just over a mile, which made it perfect for doing mile intervals. It was a little early in the season for the team to do a workout, but the boys trusted Dower and didn't question him.

Most of the path was shaded by trees, which made it great to run along in hot weather. The black top path that surrounded the lake had never completely connected because of a tributary from where the pond drained. When they arrived they were met with a horrible surprise: a bridge had been built over the tributary.

Dower walked onto the bridge as if to test it out. His face

seemed to fill with joy as he spread out his arms. "Now we can do timed distance runs here and consecutive intervals," he said.

Such sentences induced feelings of nausea in the young runners.

38

THE HIGH FROM CAMP DIDN'T last long nor did the cool weather. The warm, humid temperatures returned with the first day of school.

John always looked forward to the first day of school, but it was different that year. Julian's death had hardened him. He walked through the halls with a slower, more determined stride. Some of the girls made a stir about his long hair, but the stone look on his face still did not break. Other kids looked at him with pity. John knew what they were thinking: *They felt sorry for him because his best friend was gone.* But these looks did not help him nor did their sympathy. Their looks enraged him. He wished they would just go about their business. John did not need their sympathy. He did his best to ignore the stares and avoid talking about it. The day passed slowly, but it passed.

The Atlantic cross country team met on the back baseball field before practice. It was out of the way and, to make matters worse, the team's spot wasn't even near the bleachers—they would have to sit on the grass and fight for the shade of a nearby tree.

The team quieted down as Dower approached them. Dower began his speech the same way he had for the last thirty years.

He cleared his throat quietly. "This group will only get smaller as the season goes on." It was the perfect introduction for getting at the essence of cross country in a single sentence. The sport was only for the strong and most newcomers didn't last more than a week.

Normally, the kids bubbled with excitement, but that day it was a somber scene. John sat on the grass, the hot sun beating down on his head. Dower's words passed right through him. He wanted practice to start so he could get it over with; he did not want to hear about things like county and state championships. He simply wanted to put himself through the pain and be done with it.

It was too hot to do a workout so Dower had the team run to the Pond and do another timed distance run. Dower set up a table with cups of water. If a runner didn't grab a cup, Dower would pour one over his head or splash him in the face. It was monotonous, but the shade and water made it much easier.

After the Pond, the boys ran a dozen stride-outs across the long field in front of Atlantic school. These were drills intended to improve the runners' strides. They were not run at max pace, but usually at 75-80 percent.

That night after practice John found a big manila envelope on his bed. Inside were Nike advertisements cut from running magazines, pages of inspirational quotes and pictures of runners. There was also a note:

> *John,*
> *Julian would have wanted you to have this. Good luck this season.*
>
> *Love,*
> *Mrs. Seraphine*

The note and excerpts were comforting to him. It was then

that John knew exactly what to do with all the white space on the back of the door.

39

BY THE END OF THE week, John was spent from all the running and heat. On Friday, he fell asleep in his last period, math.

"Bonds? Bonds!" Someone nudged him from behind.

John stirred.

"I hear you're gonna win the state meet," Todd Goldman whispered.

John turned around.

"John?" the teacher called. "I see you're finally awake. How about telling us the answer?"

John turned back to the front. There were algebraic expressions all over the board.

"To which one?" John asked.

The class laughed.

"To this problem," she said, pointing.

"X to the third," Goldman whispered in his ear.

"X to the third," John answered.

"Nice job, Goldman," the teacher said.

After school, he found a surprise at his locker. Shauna and her friend Samantha were waiting for him there.

"What are you doing here?" John asked.

"Nice to see you, too," Shauna said sarcastically.

John started working the combination on his lock.

"Just visiting some friends." Shauna ran her fingers through his hair. "When are you going to get a hair cut?"

John backed away.

"What's the matter?" she asked.

"Nothing."

"How come you haven't called me at all this week?"

"I've been busy. And I can't talk now. I have to go to practice." John grabbed the books he needed and slammed his locker shut. "Look, if you want to check up on me, you could make it a little less obvious." He walked away briskly.

That day was the first real workout, the 2-2. It had been named the 2-2 because it was a giant loop around the school that was 2.2 miles long. The varsity runners had to do three timed intervals at top speed.

The 2.2 was not just the first workout of the season, it signified much more. It was considered the battlefield, and any runner approaching it would either fight or step off.

A storm came into the region and it was dark and windy that entire day. As the runners assembled outside, it looked as if it was going to rain at any moment. But practice was only canceled if there was thunder or lightning. Rain just added to the experience.

The workout started on the front field. Dower had brought out a huge clock, like the ones used in races.

"Coach, will that thing be okay in the rain?" Benji asked.

"Not sure. Line up, boys!" Dower said as he took a little starter pistol out of his jacket.

"Don't shoot!" Brett joked and held up his hands.

Everyone laughed except Dower. Then with no warning, Dower quickly fired the pistol straight into the air.

"That means go!" he shouted at a few freshmen who didn't take the hint. He shook his head at the assistant coach. "Freshmen."

John and the other varsity runners ran the first interval at a good pace, finishing together.

After the short rest interval, Dower said, "Okay, let's pick it up on this one."

Early in the second interval, John dropped back. He had a stitch. John felt like someone had put a giant staple in his side. The pain soon spread to his right shoulder. It was intense, and forced his rib cage and surrounding muscles to contract. It was hard to breathe, which made it difficult to run properly. His stride shortened and his arms—a runner's gas pedal—stopped moving. He slowed down some more.

John's first instinct was to fight the pain. He started a burst back towards the varsity group, but the pain was too much. He became frustrated and angry. All he wanted was to catch back up with the group.

It was then John remembered something Julian had taught him. He relaxed his breathing and slowed down a bit, which helped him. Then he shut his eyes and imagined himself running faster, freer, and painless, but the pain brought him back. He tried again, going back to the place where pain did not exist. He saw Julian's face. *Don't give up, John. You can do it.* This time, a deep chill came over him.

John opened his eyes, and while the pain was still there, it had decreased. He began to accelerate with small, smooth increases in his stride and speed. With each stride the pain dug into him, but he did not back down. Soon, he was running as fast as he was before the stitch set in. John began passing some of the runners.

At the mile mark, he saw Benji. John moved closer and within two blocks he passed him. Next was Lowell. Then he caught Brett and Alex with a half-mile to go. Pedro and Simon were running the lead together and John caught them at the back of the school. The three finished together.

"Nice finish, boys!" Dower yelled.

During the last loop, it started to pour. The varsity stuck together and all finished at once. Dower was now wearing a large poncho. He stared at the soaked, tired, pissed-off looks on the faces of his runners and grinned. "There will be no practice tomorrow. Enjoy it because from then on you will have practice or a race every Saturday until the season is over. And one more thing; when you go home tonight, don't forget to tell your parents you love them."

When John got home the first thing he did was fall asleep. He woke up an hour and a half later to the phone ringing and great hunger pangs.

"Do you want to come over for dinner?" Shauna asked.

"Sure," John said, still half asleep.

"Okay, I'll pick you up in a half-hour."

Shauna had just gotten her driver's license and was eager to drive anywhere. Her mom was an excellent cook, and John stuffed down two full plates of pasta with sausage and broccoli. Shauna had decided they would go get a movie and John didn't argue as that was about all he had energy for. At Blockbuster, Shauna moved through the aisles quickly and they eventually split up. When John found her, she was talking to a group of Irvington runners, including Shawn Gunther. Gunther nodded at John. John nodded back. He wasn't interested in talking to any of them.

After they walked away, John said, "I didn't know you were good friends with those guys."

"We go to the same school," she told him.

They lay on her couch in their normal spots, but it soon became apparent to John that something was very wrong. He didn't mention it and hoped she wouldn't either. John just wanted the movie to be over so he could leave.

But it happened as soon as the movie was over. Shauna looked at him seriously and said, "John, we need to talk."

He knew what was coming.

"I think we should break up," she said.

John sat silent a moment. As far as he was concerned they were already broken up—he hadn't had any real emotion towards her for nearly a month.

"Yeah," He finally said. "I guess that's what's best."

She offered to drive him home.

"Nah, I'll walk."

"In this weather?"

"It stopped raining a while ago."

For once Shauna didn't argue with him.

As he walked, a strong breeze blew from the northeast. John stiffened up as it passed through his long sleeve t-shirt and slammed right into his core.

<u>40</u>

FARTLEK, A GERMAN WORD THAT means *speed play*, certainly was a strange name for a workout, but it was an essential part of Dower's training regime.

During these runs, the team would do bursts anywhere from twenty seconds to two minutes in the middle of the run. Sometimes, Dower would tell them to do twelve to sixteen bursts. Other times, he made them do it for twenty-five minutes, with one minute on and two minutes off.

The captain would lead the workout, but the Atlantic tradition held that the captain could select anyone to lead a burst. And if any runner fell back, he was punished by having to do another burst.

This was Brett and Pedro's favorite workout, an easy way to torture the younger runners.

"Go again," Brett told Lowell.

Lowell protested, but ultimately complied.

"You, too," Pedro said to Benji.

Benji got a sour look on his face, but complied again. When he returned, Brett told him to go yet again. Benji smiled, thinking he was kidding this time.

"I'm not kidding," Brett said.

"Come on, he's fine," Simon said.

Towards the end of the workout, Brett and Pedro kept stopping short. Simon and the others slow-jogged and waited for them the first few times. But after that, Simon and John started getting mad.

"Guys, you can't just stop short," Simon complained.

"Well, your bursts are too long," Pedro shot back at him.

"Look, this is the way the workout is supposed to be done."

"A burst is a burst," Brett said, using his convoluted logic.

"Just finish the workout, you wuss's," John demanded.

Brett and Pedro ignored them and fell back, finishing the run without the main pack.

41

SATURDAY PRACTICES BEFORE THE MEETS began were common for the Atlantic runners. That weekend, Dower had to go away for a wedding and the assistant coach was sick so the team was on its own.

The workout was at Hemon Park. The park was a rectangle and the perimeter was a mile long. It wasn't a very exciting place to train, but there was lots of grass, and the loop could easily be shortened to fit any distance under a mile.

The workout that day was a 3-2-1, which was a three-mile interval followed by a two-mile interval, and then a mile. Each interval was to be run at a slightly faster pace.

When John arrived, everyone was there except Brett. He still had not arrived after they stretched and did a warm up loop, so they began their workout without him.

Brett finally arrived in the middle of the first interval and jumped in on the second mile.

"Where were you?" Simon asked.

"Sorry, my mom didn't wake me up."

"That's what an alarm clock is for," Alex said.

"Mind your own business," Brett snapped and elbowed Alex in the arm.

The force of the blow made Alex trip and fall over on the concrete. The group slowed down.

"Jesus, Brett," Simon said. He told the others to keep running while he attended to Alex.

No one said a word for the rest of the interval. When they finished, John saw Alex by the water fountain, using the water to wash the blood from his elbow.

"You okay?" John asked.

"Yeah, it's just a scrape."

"All he needs is a Band-Aid," Brett said.

Simon walked towards Brett, frowning. "What is the matter with you?"

"It was his fault."

"No it wasn't." Simon raised his voice. "And if he gets hurt we have a major problem, Brett!"

"Whatever, get out of my face," Brett said, pushing Simon away.

The anger that had been building up inside John released. He charged towards Brett.

"What's your problem?" John asked.

"Now, you want to start up, too?" Brett said.

John got in his face. The two locked stares. The others watched in awe. Brett was the biggest boy there and most of the guys were scared of him. John wasn't much smaller though, and the others knew he was strong and tough.

"You better cut the crap or there's going to be a real problem," John warned.

"Okay, tough guy," Brett mocked.

John was livid. "Everything's a joke, Brett, right? Well, you touch him again and the joke's gonna be on you."

"Whatever," Brett shrugged.

Simon stepped in between them. "Come on guys, time to start the next interval."

The group didn't say a word. Midway into the next interval

John took off from the pack. He used his anger as fuel, the rage propelling him towards the finish. John had hoped it would be a cleansing ritual, but it did not fully work.

42

THE REAL TORTURE BEGAN WITH mile intervals at the Pond, a staple every Monday. The varsity usually did five intervals with short rest periods.

At the start of the workout, John took off his lacrosse shorts to expose the little running shorts he had on underneath. Brett howled like a drunk would at a teenage girl.

John led most of the intervals around the Pond. He liked running there because of the shade and, since the trail curved, it gave the illusion the loop was shorter than its actual distance.

When they were finished, Dower recorded the varsity times, taking John's last.

"5:51, 5:45, 5:28—"

The other varsity runners turned and stared at him. It was rare for someone to run under 5:30, which was under a 5:00 minute mile.

"Go on," Dower said, not missing a beat.

43

OF ALL THE ARDUOUS WORKOUTS and places to train, Cedar Park was the worst. There was no sun coverage, so on hot days it was brutal. The park was directly on the water so there was usually a nice breeze. But later in the fall, when it turned cooler, the breeze turned into a vicious wind that cut like a knife.

There was one main reason the team went there: hill training. There were three large hills on the grass field. The team would run a half mile loop that included these three hills. If that was not enough, the park was almost three miles away from the school. The run to Cedar Park constituted a nice warm up, but the run home was no fun.

The team was lucky that day; they were not doing intervals but a modified Fartlek run. They would do about 45 minutes on the hills, doing several long, gradual bursts.

John looked over the park before they started. Just a year before, it had been the first practice he attended. Dower and the others were amazed by his ability to keep up with the varsity runners during the workout.

Shortly after, Dower started them off. Though the pace was not very intense, the heat was. The group spread out towards the middle of the run. John fell back a little. It wasn't the hills that were bothering him as much as the heat. Dower stared at him as he finished up and went right for the water. John prepared to be scolded.

But Dower surprised him, "Bonds, when are you going to cut that hair?"

44

THE FIRST RACE WAS AT Bethpage. It was a quad meet, a small meet where Atlantic ran against three other teams in the same division. The Indian summer was still haunting the runners, and the sweat was already pouring down their faces.

"This is it, boys, this is it," Dower said. "Time to show everyone what you were doing the last three months." Dower told them that none of the teams they were running against would give them any real competition. His instructions were to stay together as long as they could.

After their warm up, Dower motioned for the team to gather around. Dower reached into his pocket and took out a handful of black ribbons. "I want each of you to put one of these on your jersey. Remember, you're not just running for yourselves this season." He waited for the runners to pin them on. "Now, let's have a moment of silence."

The boys jogged across the large Polo field where the race began and lined up.

Boom!

The Atlantic runners blasted off the starting line, forming a pack towards the end of the field. Bethpage was a flat course, so the biggest challenge was the sand. John had learned to run on the edge of the course to find firmer ground while watching his teammates the prior year. The bulk of the course went through the woods, but at many points the sun shined through.

The team stayed in a pack at the lead for just over a mile. Then John started to move ahead. He felt great and kept opening up his stride as he raced along. Soon, the breathing and footstep sounds of the others were gone and he was alone in the woods. It didn't seem like a race anymore, but more like a distance run.

The woodsy trail emptied onto the same polo field where the race had begun.

The assistant grabbed Dower and said, "First man, Coach."

"Already?"

John didn't hear the small cheers as he raced across the field. When he looked back, he saw there was no one challenging him, but he finished hard anyway.

Pedro out-kicked Simon for second place, Brett was fourth, Alex was fifth, Lowell was seventh, and Benji came in nineteenth.

"Did we win?" Benji asked Dower after he finished, still huffing and puffing.

"Win?" Dower laughed. "We had five guys finish before any of the other teams had one. It was a shutout."

On the bus ride home, everyone was happy and joked around. Even John was gregarious, enjoying the cookies Julian's mother had baked for them.

FALL

Although the fall arrives each year without fail, the initial dawning is always unprecedented as if it was the first time the event had ever occurred in history. Energy—long stored at the heart of Mother Nature—explodes, splashing everything in its wake with yellow, orange, red and copper. It is the climax of the year, the divine essence making itself known to human eyes. Wild emotions are sent through the blood and the earth is sent into a wild, tumultuous spin.

45

JOHN HAD LEFT HIS WINDOWS open the night before and awoke to cool air that had planted itself all around him.

It was the first big Saturday race, an invitational at the Meadow. Invitational meets were much larger than regular quad meets. Depending on the meet, there could be more than a hundred teams, some from other states. That day, there were so many teams that there would be four varsity races.

When the Atlantic team arrived, a myriad of different colored team jerseys already swarmed the Meadow. "You couldn't ask for a better day to run," Dower said as he led the team to their spot, a large shaded area that would serve as the team's headquarters.

Atlantic was in the third race. As John and the others waited, runners and coaches came over to talk to them, shake hands and offer their condolences. John noticed a few boys running by and pointing at him.

Dower put his arm around John's shoulder. "You know why these guys are pointing at you?"

John shook his head.

"You're one of the guys they know they need to beat."

Dower brought the team into a huddle before the race.

"You know this course like you know your own backyards. Stay with the leaders until Cardiac, and then start to increase your position." The words came out so casually that it almost made John smile and lose his focus.

Boom!

The race started on a huge field of grass, which emptied into a small path or what many called the chute. The chute was a narrow path bordered by a fence and a steep hillside. It was very hard to pass runners on the chute. Position had to be secured on the field. Because of this, the Atlantic runners made sure not to go out too slow. John used his elbows to help him secure a good position on the front field. The others followed suit and all exited the field near the head of the group.

At the mile mark, the trail opened up. The crowd cheered and yelled.

"Stay exactly where you are!" Dower shouted as his runners passed him.

The initial rush of adrenaline would then calm as the runners entered the back woods, away from the crowd. Here those who had started too fast would fall back.

There wasn't any advanced strategy for racing at the Meadow. Cardiac was the major determining factor of the race. If someone had a good lead on you before Cardiac, it was unlikely you would catch them after the big hill. Since the Atlantic runners trained at the Meadow, they had a huge advantage.

John and Simon were following two runners who were leading the race when Cardiac came into view. John and Simon exchanged glances before the hill, and then burst towards the hill, overtaking the two other runners. John and Simon knew every curve and crack of that hill and could run up it blind. They increased their lead as they summited.

On the back slope, John moved ahead of Simon. His long stride and quick turnover made him particularly good at running downhill. The momentum carried him through to the end of the brush, where again he passed the crowd. Dower yelled for him to kick.

The burning in his legs and stomach went away as he came towards the final stretch. The cheering and excitement from the crowd blocked out all his pain. He did not feel how much he had exerted himself until after he crossed the line and started to walk.

Simon finished fifteen seconds behind John for second. Pedro kicked hard and took fifth place. Brett came in twelfth and Alex twenty second. Lowell finished thirty-ninth—he had gotten a bad cramp—and Benji was seventy-eighth after going out way too hard. The five man total was forty-two.

Dower did some quick calculations with the assistant coach and said he believed the team had won. Not long after, the official results were calculated and it was announced that Atlantic had won. John's time was the fastest of the day.

The boys had to wait for the girls races before they could leave. Dower instructed them to cheer for the girls, but most of them just slept under the tree. Later on, the Baldwin girl's team stopped by. Alex and a few of the others began to talk to them. John peered out from under his hood and saw Leah standing there. She had just finished racing—her hair was a little sweaty, face flushed—but he thought she still looked gorgeous. John thought about getting up and saying hi. But before John could stand up, they jogged away.

46

AS IF IT WERE NOT enough to have an entire day with nothing to do, Sunday nights were endless. John used to spend the long hours talking to Shauna on the phone, but he had not spoken to her in over a week. There was nothing on TV. He put on some music, laid on his bed and stared at the ceiling. Thoughts began to come slowly and cyclically like the turning of a great wheel. With each turn he was met with the pain and suffering of losing his best friend, the weight of the predicament he was in and the pressure he felt to succeed. All he had to look forward to was another long week of school and practice.

47

THE FIRST IMPORTANT RACE FOR the team was a quad meet against Oceanside. Oceanside had won the county title the year before. And although their best runner, Sutton, was gone, they still had a strong team. Their team's new best runner was actually a sophomore, a prodigy on the track. Dower believed he was the number one contender for the county title. None of the other runners on that team were standouts, but the team had a lot of depth and strong coaching, and always managed to produce strong runners every season.

Dower matched up the Atlantic runners to the Oceanside runners, like man-to-man defense in basketball. Each boy knew who he had to beat.

Boom!

The race went out at a blistering pace. The Oceanside runners were not content to follow and the Atlantic runners could not allow them to lead. They jockeyed for position, switching back and forth.

John stayed with the sophomore. He went out hard and took the lead. John let him lead for a while, then ran alongside him. At the mile and a half mark, the sophomore surged. It was a long burst designed to break John, but he held tight. After the burst, the boy did not fade. He slowed down, but stayed consistent at a fast pace.

At the two-mile mark, John put in a burst. The boy tried to hold him off. John backed off a little and pretended to be fatigued. A minute later, he did another burst, this one even faster. They went head-to-head for what seemed like a long distance, and then the boy began breathing very loudly. Finally, John broke him.

John shot out of the woods with a narrow lead, but on the polo field he buried the sophomore. His stride lengthened and he tore across the grass, his lead increasing and increasing as they went. John managed to put nearly twenty seconds on the boy by the finish.

Simon was next, and though he kicked hard, he did not catch the sophomore and took third. Pedro kicked hard and managed to get fourth place, beating Oceanside's second best runner. Brett and Alex were next, only letting one runner between them. Atlantic had won.

Dower was so thrilled that he took the kids out for pizza after the meet. As John walked home, Dower's Jeep pulled up next to him.

"15:42. The fastest time last year was 15:53. That was by Julian when he beat Sutton," Dower happily informed. "Keep this up and you're not just going to be a contender for the county title, but for the state title, Bonds."

48

THE POND HAD BEEN PAINTED and the black path that surrounded it was now a mesh of yellows and oranges. The back woods looked like a distant, surreal place.

In the two weeks that followed, Atlantic won another four races—two quad meets and two small invitationals. John had won all of them. *Newsday* came down to take a team picture and printed an article titled "Atlantic's Back" in their sports section, which talked about Julian's death and the team's mission.

Larger turnouts started to appear at the meets—more parents, more students and even a few faculty members. The bus was so packed with kids that the freshman had to triple up. (Of course, the varsity seniors had their own seats.) After the races the runners were met with cookies, fruit, and offers to be taken to dinner. Though John enjoyed fine free dining, he passed on many offers, preferring to be alone with some deli food and beer.

49

Dower was the only one not caught up in all the excitement. There was something that concerned him.

Before practice that day, Dower decided to address the team. "Though we have had a great start, I don't want any of you to get overconfident. We still have a long way to go. Though we beat Oceanside, we still have not raced Irvington. But I believe we have a bigger problem. There's a large gap between our first five runners and our sixth and seventh," Dower pointed out ruefully.

"A team is only as good as its fifth man. It did not matter how fast our first, second, third or fourth runners are—our fifth man could lose the race for the team."

"Someone is going to have to step up. I don't know who that person is, but one of you is going to have to."

50

As if to make Dower's prophecy come true, the next week, Lowell started to complain of extreme pain in his shins. Shin splints were a disaster, a curse for a distance runner. It felt like someone was driving a spike into your shin as it hit the concrete, and the only cure was to gradually cut your mileage until the inflammation calmed down. If that didn't work, the runner would have to stop running altogether.

That same week, Alex had also complained about his Achilles tendon. Dower had no choice but to sit them both out during the quad meet on the Wednesday of that week. It was not a big deal, since the quad meet had no real impact on the big races, but Dower wasn't pleased.

"Why aren't you two racing?" Brett asked again, not comprehending why the two of them were not in uniform.

"His shins hurt and I need another day of recovery," Alex replied.

"Recovery from what?"

"The workouts."

"You both need to recover from being wusses!" Pedro teased.

Doc had come down to watch the meet and noticed that Lowell and Alex weren't running.

"These guys are always getting hurt," Doc pointed out. "We weren't allowed to get injured."

Dower nodded. "And these guys don't even run half the mileage you guys did."

"Mother's philosophy," Doc said.

Dower looked at him curiously.

Doc pushed, "The mother's philosophy goes like this: If something hurts, you shouldn't do it. If you're tired, you should rest. If the weather's bad, you should stay inside. If something's too hard, you quit."

Dower broke in, "Sure rings true today."

Doc continued, "The mother's philosophy is the antithesis of the philosophy of the warrior. For the warrior, pain, suffering and toil are holy and worshipped as great values. Our parents and grandparents were tough. They had to work for everything they had. They had to be tough. But today, these kids were given everything and didn't have to work for it."

"Kids sure aren't as tough as they used to be," Dower agreed as he screamed at a few of his runners.

John, Simon, Brett, Pedro and Benji stayed in a pack and won the race easily, taking places one through five.

"That freshman is really becoming a runner, huh, Coach?" Doc asked.

"Sure is. In fact, he reminds me of another freshman prodigy I coached."

"Who's that?"

"You. Except you were much more of a nerd."

51

Of all the Atlantic parties, homecoming was always the biggest and craziest party of the year. It took John a long time to convince Simon to come to the party. Simon didn't want anyone to go since there was a race the next day. After much cajoling, John got him to agree. But Simon swore he would not stay long.

Not long after they arrived at the party, Simon noticed John, Brett and Pedro drinking. Simon filled with rage.

"What do you guys think you are doing?"

"What?" Pedro asked.

"Atlantic tradition," Brett said.

Simon stared at John.

"You think this is okay?"

John shrugged. "I'm just having one."

Simon shook his head. "All you guys do is think about yourselves." He stormed off.

"What's up his butt?" Brett asked John.

"He's just nervous about the race tomorrow," Pedro said.

A little later, Pedro grabbed John's arm. "Come on! Irvington's here! You won't believe this!"

John followed him to the back of the party, where Shauna was talking to Jim Patole, from Irvington. Some of the other Irvington guys were there too, including Shawn Gunther. John bolted towards her.

"What are you doing here?" he asked Shauna.

"What? I can't come to my friend's party?"

"You know what I mean, Shauna."

"What did you think? I wasn't going to find out about that girl at camp?"

"What are you talking about?"

"You think I'm stupid? I have my sources."

"Now I see what this is about," John said, smiling at Patole. "You can have her."

Patole smiled back.

"Let's kick his ass," Brett yelled.

John thought about it. But he knew one punch and his season was over. He shook his head. "No, we'll settle this on the course, like men."

Brett looked at Shauna as he turned away to follow John. "Ho!"

What was supposed to be a mild night turned into a wild night. John got himself drunk and started hitting on all the younger girls with Brett and Pedro. Brett found a set of football shoulder pads, a helmet, and a jersey upstairs, in the boy's room that was having the party. He came down and started tackling people.

The three ended up sleeping over. Brett slept in the master bedroom upstairs with a senior girl. Pedro and John took the couches downstairs.

When John woke up, it was light out. He looked at a clock and saw they only had twenty minutes to be at the school. He nudged Pedro.

"Get up, we're gonna be late," John said.

Pedro sat up dizzily. "Late for what?"

"The meet, idiot."

Luckily, the house was not far from the school. The three walked as fast as they could. When they arrived all their teammates were already dressed and ready to go. Brett opened his locker and realized he had left his racing sneakers at home. He had no choice but to tell Dower.

Finding racing sneakers for Brett wasn't easy since he was a size 13½. Dower asked the JV runners and finally found a freshman who had size 13. Ironically, he was a short boy, only about 5'1".

"You got some big feet for a little guy," Dower said to the freshman.

"You know what they say about guys with big feet," Brett said as he grinned towards the freshman.

"Yeah, they have small brains," Dower said.

52

THE RACE WAS A HUGE invitational at Van Cortland Park. It was the most competition the team had faced yet. The course was only 2.5 miles as opposed to the normal 5K courses they ran, so it was normally a very fast race. It was not a hard course, but it was one of the most dangerous; there were large rocks scattered all over the trails and it was very easy for a runner to twist his ankle if he wasn't paying attention.

Simon did not say a word to the others before the race. John, Brett and Pedro were tired and were also quiet. The other boys made small talk and didn't seem to know what was going on.

Dower instructed the boys to go out a little faster than they normally would since it was difficult to pass runners at the beginning of the race. Like the Meadow course, the Van Cortland course started on a large field but quickly emptied into a narrow pass only a few feet wide. Some kids were pushed into the brush, others tripped on the large rocks.

It was cold out. John's muscles were stiff and he felt he may not have warmed up enough as he stood on the line.

Boom!

John shot off the line and went towards the front of the field. He made it to the chute safely, staying close to the other leaders.

The dirt on the course was hard, almost like concrete. John couldn't find his rhythm. Before he knew it, the leaders were out of sight, and Simon had caught him.

John and Simon ran together for a little while. John passed him on the long, gradual downhill before the final quarter-mile stretch. John darted towards the finish, but had kicked too late. He only passed two runners for a seventh place finish.

Simon was ninth. Alex had gone out too slow and finished twenty-first. Pedro had gotten a second wind in the last half-mile and made up some ground for twenty-third, and Benji was fifth man in forty-fifth. Lowell wasn't far back in fifty-first. Brett ran horribly, coming in far behind the others, finishing in the 100's.

Overall, the team didn't do so badly. They were third in their race and only one of the teams that beat them was from New York. Still, there were other varsity races that day, and many teams performed much better than Atlantic. Dower wasn't pleased.

Simon led the team on a cool down in the back woods, away from all the people. On the back trails, a small rock cliff was visible.

"Hey look at that," Alex said. He pointed to a large flat rock spray-painted with *Atlantic XC, 1985.*

"I know who did that," Brett said.

"Who?" Alex asked.

"Jack Irons."

"How do you know?"

"My brother told me."

"How did they get up there?" Pedro asked.

"I don't know, but let's go check it out," Brett suggested.

"Guys, lets just do our cool down," Simon said.

Everyone except Simon stopped to check out the cliff. He continued the run on his own.

The team ended up walking back. Before they reached their camp, the team crossed paths with the Baldwin girls. The girls didn't need much of a reason to stop running and the teams began to talk.

This time John approached Leah without hesitation. Before he could say anything she playfully took his hood off. "Your hair got long," she said.

If anyone else had made the comment it would have angered him, but with her it was ok.

"I saw your picture in the paper…I mean…I saw your name in the paper. You guys are doing awesome."

They made small talk until the others were ready to leave.

"Can I call you some time?" John asked.

"Okay," Leah replied without hesitation.

Though John didn't run well, he rode the bus home in a good mood.

53

Sometimes the impact of losing a race was much more powerful than the one from winning. Monday Dower seemed happier, almost relieved, as he walked across the field with his clipboard.

"I have seen it built up too many times before. A team on a winning streak folds under pressure," Dower said. "Losing can be a good thing sometimes…especially if you learn from it."

"Our mission this season is not to win every meet. It's to win the ones that count. Because of this, we are training through our remaining races. We will be running practices on days before meets. See you at the Pond."

As John ran the first two mile intervals at the Pond, he didn't feel as strong as he normally did. His legs were still sore from the race that weekend. John finished the third mile at the back of the varsity group.

Dower studied him like an FBI agent focusing on a terrorist. "John, take the next interval off."

John sucked up the pain and finished the last mile at the head of the varsity group. Dower gave him a nod, but he still felt weary.

54

THE NEXT DAY, JOHN WOKE up to an unpleasant surprise: He was sick. He took off practice Tuesday, but Wednesday Dower wanted him to run in the quad meet.

Dower came up to him before the meet.

"You'll take it easy today. Stick with Benji or Lowell. Same goes for the next few days, then you'll be back."

The race was at New York Institute of Technology. It was a hilly course and much tougher than Bethpage. John disliked the course because it had lots of twists and turns. He found it disrupted his rhythm. This course was where the county meet would be held.

John stayed back, running with Lowell for most of the race. And with little competition, Atlantic won the meet easily.

55

EVERY YEAR THE RUNNERS WENT on an overnight trip to the Schenectady Invitational in Upstate New York. The bus didn't leave until after third period on Friday and John took the opportunity to sleep late. But he wasn't the only one with the same idea. Simon, Pedro and Brett also cut their first three classes.

Normally, this wouldn't be a problem. The dean was the wrestling coach and was lenient on varsity athletes. But the new vice principal had become wise to it. He was not as supportive of sports and kept a close eye on the dean. This day, the vice principal realized what was going on and alerted the main principal.

As the four runners lay on the gym mats waiting to leave, they were called into the principal's office. They, the vice principal, the dean and Dower all crammed into the head principal's office.

The dean looked at the runners. "Did you guys go to your first three classes?"

No one answered. Dower shook his head. "I told each of you, you had to attend the first three periods."

The assistant principal looked at Dower. "Well, Coach, it's very simple then. They're not going to the Invitational."

Dower looked back in disbelief. The dean and principal

sensed what was about to happen and asked the boys to go into the hallway. They shut the door behind them.

What followed after was a loud shouting match. A few minutes later, Dower and the dean walked out. Dower nodded at him as they split up.

Red-faced, Dower turned to the runners and said, "Two weeks detention when you get back and if you miss another class, you will be suspended and off the team. And you better be silent on the bus ride up." Then he stormed off.

There was only one hotel close to the meet, and it was where most of the teams who were traveling stayed. After the team unpacked and changed, they headed to the course for a short run before dinner.

The temperature was cold, in the high thirties, and it was supposed to get even colder overnight. It was two hours before dusk, but seemed later. Dower instructed them to run the course twice.

On the first loop, the team passed a large statue of a kneeling man. The man looked like he was about to receive an honor or be blessed.

"This is where you kick, Benji," Simon said.

On the second loop, Pedro and Brett made it clear that they wanted to take a shortcut back.

Simon refused.

"Dower's not gonna know," Pedro responded. "It's freezing."

"I don't care," Brett said. "I'm going back."

Simon looked at John for support. John hesitated.

"It's freezing out here," John said.

Pedro and Brett turned onto the shortcut. The group stopped.

Simon looked at them. "If you guys want to you can, but I'm not cutting the loop."

He jogged off, accompanied only by Benji.

"Where are Simon and Benji?" Dower asked the group when they returned without them.

"We split up," Pedro said quickly.

"Why?" Dower asked bluntly.

"Because we were cold," Pedro replied.

Dower was furious. "What kind of team leaves their captain? That's ridiculous. Get on the bus. I don't want to look at any of you for the rest of the night."

Dower waited outside in the cold for Simon and Benji to return.

The team ate dinner at the restaurant inside the hotel. Dower was true to his word and ate dinner in the bar with another coach while the assistant coach watched over the team.

At dinner, John realized the Baldwin girls' team was also staying at the hotel. John saw Leah on the other side of the restaurant. Busy talking to her teammates, Leah either didn't see him or was ignoring him. But after dinner, Alex's girlfriend came over to the table and slipped Alex a note.

"What's it say?" Brett demanded.

"Tell you soon," Alex said, pointing to the assistant coach.

After dinner, the team had a secret meeting in Alex's room.

"They want us to meet up with them later," Alex said.

"Sweet," Brett said, hugging Alex and lifting him off the ground.

"Wow, Alex, when did you become cool?" John said.

The team waited for Dower to check up on them before they did anything. Dower always made sure all the boys were in their rooms at curfew, which was 9:00 pm. But because Dower was angry with them, he asked the assistant coach to check in on them. After he left, the boys got ready to go out.

Simon was lying on the bed in his sweats when Alex and the others showed up at his room.

Alex looked at Simon with furrowed brows. "You're not coming?"

"Nope."

"He doesn't like girls," Brett said.

"No, unlike you Brett, I actually care about the race tomorrow."

"Calm down, dude," Pedro said.

"No, I'm not gonna calm down. It's going to be another Van Cortland."

John tried to calm Simon down.

"Si, what are we gonna do? Go to bed at 9:00?"

Simon wouldn't budge.

"Watch, he's gonna tell," Pedro said as they walked out.

The girls wanted to hang out by the pool, but the Atlantic boys knew that was too obvious. They found a better area—a large conference room on the top floor.

The Baldwin varsity girls were serious and did not party before meets. But the guys were deviants and had brought alcohol with them. They told some other kids and soon it turned into a full blown party.

John was adamant about not partaking in the drinking that time, but Brett and Pedro couldn't resist. Although he tried to stop them, he found himself distracted by Leah. They started to talk and John soon became oblivious to everything else going on in the room.

Later in the night, some of the kids wanted to go in the pool.

John stayed back with Leah on a soft, comfortable couch in the room. Someone jokingly shut off the lights as they left. The two sat close and John could smell her perfume. It immediately reminded him of camp. He apologized about what had happened at camp, explaining the real situation as best he could. Leah stopped him before he could finish with a kiss.

They kissed for a long time, and then Leah told him it was time to go to bed.

John walked her back to her room and, on the way back,

they passed the pool. The others were still swimming and were also very loud.

"Guys, we got to race tomorrow," John reminded them.

At that moment, Pedro picked John up and tried to throw him in the pool, but John fought him off. Then Brett grabbed him from behind, clutching him tight. He put all his weight into John and finally tackled him into the pool. Leah thought she was fine until the girls grabbed her.

If John wasn't in such a good mood, he would have decked both of them, but instead he and Leah laughed and swam with the others for a little while before they went to bed.

56

THE ALARM CLOCK WOKE JOHN out of a deep sleep and he felt like he had only slept an hour or two.

Five minutes later, there was a knock at the door. Simon answered it and Dower walked in.

"Well, *there's* a surprise. Thought I'd have to break the door down to get you four up." He paused. "What's that smell?"

"Brett's sneakers," John answered.

"All of you downstairs in fifteen," Dower demanded.

It was a few degrees above freezing. The wind cut through John's wind pants like a sharp blade. Most of the varsity fell asleep during the bus ride to the course, though it was only twenty minutes away.

The team did a short warm-up. The cold was brutal and John felt tired and stiff even after the run. When they came back, Dower gave them a brief pep talk.

Schenectady was a competitive meet, but Atlantic usually won it. Dower pointed out the teams and runners they would most likely have to worry about.

"Okay, go get 'em!" Dower shouted, patting Pedro and Brett

hard on the back. Both looked as if they were going to throw up.

Boom!

Brett fell back first, near the half-mile point. Not long afterward, he started dry heaving and hobbled off the course.

At the mile mark, John knew he was in trouble. He had not gone out that fast, but his breathing was erratic and the cold air was stinging his lungs. His extremities were cold and his legs felt heavy. He seemed to be working much harder than normal, but still not moving very fast.

Soon, Simon passed him, then Alex. John tried to go with them, but found he couldn't. He became frustrated and angry, and tried to fight the fatigue. But the fighting only seemed to make him weaker. Runners kept going by him. The pain and weakness only intensified. He wanted to stop—to walk, but as horrible as he felt, a part of him would not let him stop.

The course was only 2.5 miles, but it seemed an eternity before he reached the statue where the Atlantic runners had been instructed to start their kicks. The statue looked different from the day before. The day before he thought the man was strong and proud. But now, he seemed more like a man pleading for mercy and forgiveness.

John wanted the pain to go away and called on God to help him. He begged and prayed for the pain to go away. No help came. John cursed God, and then himself.

John managed to speed up a little before the finish, but was only able to pass one runner.

No one from the team ran well. Atlantic was fourth overall in a meet they had won almost every year they attended it. There were so many reasons for Dower to be mad that he seemed to have a mental overload. All his emotional responses seemed to shut off and all he managed to say in a dull, eerie manner was, "Go cool down."

John didn't look at Dower or make eye contact with any of

the others as he dressed. He put his hood up, not wanting anyone to see or notice him.

During the cool down no one on the team said a word. After they were finished John, Brett and Pedro went to the bus and slept during the girls and JV races, although they were supposed to be cheering them on. When the race was over and everyone entered the bus, Dower didn't say a word to any of them. They stopped for dinner, and still, Dower remained silent.

John slept most of the ride. When he woke up, it was dark and he could see only the lights of passing cars. John felt bad about not talking to Leah during the meet or even bothering to look for her.

Dower stopped John as he walked off the bus and pulled him to the side. "What happened today?"

"I don't know, Coach."

Dower studied him. "You lost a week when you were sick. It will take another week to get it back."

Simon offered John a ride home. John accepted, but soon wished he hadn't. On the way, there was an uneasy silence.

"John?" Simon finally said as he stopped in his driveway.

John turned to him.

"We can't let them screw this up."

John nodded in agreement.

What was even more unsettling was the silence John was met with when he reached his house. As usual, his mom wasn't home and there was some food in the fridge. There was also a twelve-pack of beer. John ate the food and opened a can. He soon became bored and anxious. When he looked at the clock, he saw that it was only 7:30. John made a few phone calls and found out there was a party. Then Brett called and they decided go.

The two stayed out late and neither mentioned the race earlier that day.

During Julian's sophomore year, he went on the overnight trip to Schenectady. He was on the varsity filling in for a hurt senior. It had snowed the night before and the course was covered with a few inches of snow. Julian finished in sixteenth place as the fourth man and ran in 17:27. Atlantic destroyed the other teams that October day.

Julian's dad was waiting for him when he got off the bus.

Dower grabbed him by the shoulders and showed him off, yelling, "Mr. Seraphine, today your son became a runner!"

57

JOHN GOT UP LATE ON Sunday. He sat in the kitchen a long time, staring at the sports sections of the newspaper. It was the first race he had run that season where his time had not made the paper. John noticed another invitational, one that Irvington had run in and won.

He thought about taking a run. Outside, the wind blew around the autumn leaves. It looked cold and uninviting. John decided to put it off until later in the afternoon. Around noon, Leah called and invited him to the movies.

After the movie was over, they snuck into another movie theater, though they didn't watch much of it. When John got home it was dark and he did not go running.

Julian loved running in the afternoon, especially on Sundays. He would plan his entire day around the run—filling the earlier part of the day with inane errands, and then putting off any activity that might conflict until after.

Julian headed west slowly, leaning into the sunset, always affording himself the necessary time to let his body warm up. He would turn north after a mile, onto a long street with many crossroads. This way he could extend his route as far as he wanted and let his body judge the appropriate distance.

Julian ended his runs at the Atlantic track. He would walk a lap or two before resting on the bleachers, just in time to catch the end of the brilliant display of colors in the sky. Julian meditated on running, life, and the future until darkness crept in. He only left when he began to feel the coldness of the steel bleachers.

58

THE FINAL QUAD MEET WAS Wednesday. The first three Atlantic runners came out of the brush and John was nowhere to be found. Several other runners came out, and then finally, John.

Dower and the assistant coach didn't even recognize John as he ran to the finish along the polo field. His chest was sunken, his stride was remarkably short, and his head was down. It certainly did not look like the John Bonds who had won the first race of the season there.

Dower didn't say anything to John after the meet, nor did any of his teammates.

59

LIKE CLOCKWORK, WHEN YOU NEEDED Dower, he was nowhere to be found, and when you didn't want to see him, he suddenly appeared. John was enjoying a few fresh-baked cookies with milk in the lunchroom when Dower approached him.

"What's the matter?" Dower asked sternly.

"I don't know," John replied.

"What hurts?"

"Everything."

Dower shook his head, disappointed.

"You're going to sit out the conference meet this weekend. Go light with the team today and for the rest of the week. We're going to start cutting your mileage. A few speed workouts next week and you'll be ready for counties."

John nodded.

"Two more races, Bonds. Two more races," Dower said as he walked away frustrated.

60

FRIDAY, THE TEAM GOT A surprise visitor: Doc. The team was not in the best mood, but Doc managed to cheer them up. He told great stories about running, wild adventures he had, and his teammates in high school.

Dower pulled John aside after the run to see how he was doing.

"I'm okay, Coach," John informed.

Dower nodded.

When John went into the locker room, everyone was gone except for Doc.

"How come your locker isn't on the varsity wall?" Doc asked.

"More room over here," John said.

There was a long silence as John changed.

Finally, Doc said, "John, let's cut through all the nonsense. What's going on?"

John looked the little man over. He appeared so weak, yet there was so much power, will and strength in him. "I feel like junk, Doc. I don't know what's wrong with me." John put his head down. "I think I'm burning out."

Doc smiled. "There's no such thing as burning out, John."

"Then what's happening to me?" John asked, exasperated. "I used to lead every workout. I never got sore and I won every race. Now I can barely keep up with these guys."

"John, the workouts have just caught up with you. That's Dower's method. It's a transition period. The pain and soreness passes as you peak at the end of the season. This is how Dower has trained his runners for thirty years."

"Then why isn't this happening to the other runners?"

"It is, but most of the runners at your level are used to it by now. You're probably not because you weren't pushing it this hard last year. Listen to me," Doc said, his face turning serious as he put his hand on John's shoulder. "I want to tell you something, something I'm not sure anyone has ever said to you. John, you have more raw talent and ability than anyone who has come out of this locker room in a long time."

John looked away.

"Everyone knows this. Dower, your teammates—Julian knew it, too. But it's time you know it and accept it. Your teammates look up to you, John. I know Simon's the captain, but they don't respect him like they do you."

John finally met his stare.

"Now, I know you're tired. And, okay, you lost a few races, but who cares? No big deal, John. The best runners in the world lose races from time to time. Take two days off. You'll come back refreshed."

They walked out together.

Doc smiled. "By the way, how are things going with that girl?"

"Good," John answered.

"Enjoy it. Most of these other guys will never get a girl like that."

"Want a ride?" Doc asked.

"I'll walk."

"Good. Cause I ran here."

They shook hands and parted.

"You guys can do this," Doc said as he jogged away, "I know you can."

61

CROSS COUNTRY WAS ALWAYS ABOUT adapting to new circumstances. Courses varied, as did the weather, making for very different conditions. When it was warm, the rain was glorious to run in. But the rain at the conference meet was the worst kind of rain. The temperature was just above freezing. The runner's jerseys, shorts, skin, and hair all held water yet stayed cold. To make things even worse, it had rained so hard the night before that the course was in ruins. There was water and mud all over. The New York Tech course was also hilly, which made it even more dangerous. As Dower often said, the tougher conditions always favored the tougher runners.

Dower handed each of the varsity runners a huge set of spikes and said, "Use these. They may be illegal, but today I don't think anyone's gonna notice."

John stood with Julian's mother and watched the meet. She didn't ask him why he wasn't running. He figured Dower had said something. Either way, he knew the conference meet wasn't that important. The county meet was the big meet, which the team needed to qualify for the state meet.

The race started out slow. Brett—reckless and not a man to

179

conform to peer pressure—took the lead early in the race. But he didn't realize there was a reason the other runners were being cautious. The mud was so deep that even his big spikes didn't give him much grip. On the first big downhill, Brett fell and rolled down almost the entire section. His head came close to colliding with a tree. After that, he lost all his rhythm and began to fall back.

Still, the Atlantic team won the meet easily. Pedro and Simon took 1st and 2nd, Alex 4th, and Lowell and Benji finished in the top 20 places.

As the runners dressed, one of the mothers noticed Lowell had opened up his calf after being spiked by one of the runners.

Dower calmed her instantly, taking one look at the gash and proclaiming, "It doesn't need stitches." Then he looked at the others. "Go do a quick cool down." He sent Lowell to the bus so the assistant coach could clean him up.

That night John went over Leah's house. When Leah brought up running, John shied away from the subject. She knew he did not run in the conference meet so she didn't press the issue. John spent the rest of his weekend with her and a case of beer.

62

THE BLACK PATH HAD RESURFACED at the Pond and the colors were gone. There were just a few lone scattered amber leaves wafting around.

"This is the last time we'll be here this season," Dower said.

John's body was still hurting, nothing felt right and his stride was out of place. John's first two laps were a little slow, but the third was something different—a sign to him, the others and Dower—that something was terribly wrong.

When John finally came in to the finish, Dower tapped his own head a few times as if to say, "*It's all in your head.*" This made John furious. He walked towards the parkway and away from the others. When he came back, he noticed Dower staring at him.

"Bonds, go home," Dower said, startling John and the others.

Without saying a word, John stared back, sadly bowed his head, and walked away.

"What's wrong with him?" Benji whispered to Alex.

"He's burnt out," Pedro answered.

"Shut up," Simon replied.

John walked back to the school instead of running there. John took a different route back so no one could see him. He made sure to walk slowly so he wouldn't have to face Dower or any of his teammates when he finally got back to the locker room.

Coach Dower was a force in Atlantic. It was not just his coaching record, but his ability to touch and transform the lives of so many kids. Julian knew that had it not been for Dower's intervention, many runners—many great runners—would not have graduated. Even worse, they would have been lost to drugs or crime.

Julian witnessed many acts of kindness over the years. Dower would provide students with money to help them get to meets or buy them new running sneakers if their family could not afford it. Yet, Julian knew for each act he had witnessed in person, there were countless others. The kids who were one step from the edge, and close to losing it all. These were the kids that would never be heard about or seen again had it not been for Dower.

Julian had come to an understanding with Dower early on in his career. In exchange for his hard work and diligence, Dower would do anything in his power to help him develop to his fullest potential.

Dower asked for nothing in return, except undying devotion to the sport. He wanted nothing more than to see his boys succeed.

Most times Dower was stoic and his face hard to read. But when the team won, Dower was more ecstatic than they were. And when the team lost, he was more deeply crushed.

63

THE FOLLOWING DAY, JOHN DIDN'T show up for practice. He went straight home from school, making sure none of his teammates saw him. At practice, his teammates and Dower wondered where he was. Dower asked the other boys, but no one had any information.

The next day, when John did not show up again, Dower was visibly perplexed and so were some of the boys. Dower wanted answers, but no one seemed to know anything.

On Thursday, John saw some of his teammates during the day. They asked him if he was running in the county meet. John told them yes, and that he just needed a few days to rest. At lunch, Alex told him Dower was looking for him. John did not want to see him. After lunch he decided he would leave school early. But before he left, he stopped in the track locker room to get his sweatshirt.

When he walked in, the lights were out and he didn't bother to turn them on as he opened his locker.

"What's going on, man?" A voice startled John.

John flipped the lights on and saw Simon lying on the bench, where he had been taking a nap.

"Oh, that's bright." Simon said.

"You scared me."

Simon sat up and looked at John seriously. "Where have you been?"

John stared at him, and then turned back toward his locker.

Simon stood up and went near him. "Are you hurt?"

John grabbed his sweatshirt and shut his locker.

"You're just gonna quit, huh? Just like that, without an explanation?" Simon yelled as John turned and walked away. "Come on, man! You can't even look me in the eyes?" Simon grabbed John's jacket.

John turned around, grabbing Simon by the shirt and slamming him into the lockers. He held him there a second before he said anything.

"What are you gonna do, John? Beat me up?" Simon said.

John loosened his grip. "I'm burnt out, Si. My season's over." Then he let him go. John snatched up his bag and dashed out.

Before he went home, he went to the deli and persuaded the boss to let him purchase a twelve-pack. He drank most of it that night as he sat in his room alone.

64

FRIDAY, JOHN DIDN'T GO TO school. He stayed home and watched TV all day. In the afternoon he decided he would go to Leah's and surprise her when she came home from practice. He took a taxi there and snuck into her room easily, as the windows were open.

He was lying on her bed when she walked in.

"What are you doing here?" she asked.

"I came to surprise you." John kissed her quickly, but the smell of alcohol on his breath made her back away.

"What's the matter?" John asked.

"Started a little early today?"

He didn't respond.

"John, how come you didn't go to practice this week?"

John backed away.

"Coach told me to take a few days off."

"You're running tomorrow, right?"

"Yeah."

She gave him a sidelong look. "John, don't lie to me. I know stopped going to practice. What's going on?"

He sat down on her bed. She sat next to him and ran her hand through his hair.

"Just tell me what's wrong," Leah said in soft voice.

John took a deep breath. "That's what everyone wants to know," John said, starting to get angry. "That's what I want to know. And guess what? I don't know Leah. I don't know. "I'm burnt out, I guess."

She shook her head. "John, you're not burnt out, you just had a few bad races."

John became perplexed. "No! That's what everyone keeps saying, but it's not that simple. You don't understand," he said, walking away again.

"What do you mean?"

John turned around. "I'm done. My season's over. I have nothing left."

"John, listen to yourself. That's ridiculous. You're not taking care of yourself. All you're doing is drinking. That's not rest."

"Oh, the expert is here."

"I'm just trying to help."

"Well, you're not doing a good job."

She shook her head. "Go home."

John opened her window and climbed out. He began walking away.

"John, come back. Talk to me!" She called.

John turned, looking her in the eyes.

"You're just going to give up, just like that?" she asked.

"It's not that simple, Leah."

John walked the rest of the way home. It was dark out when he returned. There were messages from a few of the team mothers and Simon. He erased them all.

John then remembered there was a jock party that night. None of the runners would be there because of the meet the next day.

John walked into the party and went straight for the keg.

"Hey, Bonds, what did you drop, math?" Todd Goldman asked.

"Uh…yeah," John said, trying to move by.

"Hey, aren't the counties tomorrow?" Goldman asked.

John nodded.

"Drinking before a big meet!" Goldman shouted. "You runners are crazy man!"

John tried to socialize with some of the football players, but he couldn't enjoy himself. His mind kept going to dark places. He kept thinking about the meet the next day and how he let everyone down. He decided to leave the party.

As John made his way out the front door, he found a small bottle of Jack Daniels on the dining room table and slipped it under his jacket.

The party was near the school and John ended up on the bleachers, staring out at the track. As he sipped the harsh liquid, he thought about Julian and the debacle the season had become. He felt he should never have joined the team in the first place. Perhaps he should have picked soccer or football. It would have been so much easier. He didn't belong; surely he wasn't one of them. He had betrayed Julian—and everyone else who had believed in him. And he hated them all—the team, Dower, the greats, the team mothers. It was Julian who had talked him into the whole thing in the first place. It was his fault. But as much as John could blame the others and push them away, there was one person he could not get away from—the one person he hated the most—himself.

John wished he could make it all go away. But as he sat there alone, in the darkness, the pain and rage tore at him. Gulp after gulp, he drank, trying to drown out the anguish. Finally, he went numb and stumbled home.

65

JOHN WOKE UP EARLY THE next morning to a sharp pain in the left side of his head. The rest of his body felt like it had been run over by a truck. He needed fresh air so he walked to the side of his house. John was shaking and felt like throwing up, but he didn't. The cold air soothed him. He stayed outside until he was too cold to stay out any longer.

John poured a huge glass of water and took some aspirin. He sat on his bed for a long time wondering what to do. Finally, John decided to go to the meet.

There was a large turnout at the county meet. Atlantic had alumni, parents, teachers and kids in their corner. Many people asked about John. Dower acted like a politician, answering all questions calmly though he wasn't sure of all the answers. The rumors varied as the mothers whispered complicated tales that involved John's sickness and his missing weeks of practice.

Before the meet, Doc and Bruce pulled Brett aside to get to the bottom of things. But Brett could offer them no further information than what they knew already.

John took the local bus to the meet. He wore a baseball cap

and a hood over it. He stayed far from the Atlantic corner, hiding himself in the crowd of spectators.

John noticed his hands were still shaking and made sure to keep them in his pockets. John overheard some people talking. Ironically, Shawn Gunther was hurt and wasn't running in the race.

The race went off. Most of the Atlantic team stayed towards the front of the pack. The race entered into the back woods. John stayed his ground for fear that someone may see him.

It was not long before the first runner came out of the brush. It was the sophomore from Oceanside. Pedro and Simon were right behind him. Alex was third man in 11th; Lowell was 29th and Benji in 41st place. Brett choked, finishing very far back.

John noticed Several Oceanside runners finishing near the Atlantic runners. Irvington looked like they ran well, too. He knew it would be close. John waited nervously until they announced the scores. Finally, the announcement came, Atlantic had won.

John left. As he was crossing the parking lot, Leah and her team jogged past him. John put his head down, but not quick enough. One of her teammate's spotted him. She told Leah, and soon the entire group stopped. Leah walked towards him.

John's breathing quickened and blood rose to his face and neck.

"Well, I guess they didn't need you after all," she said.

He glared at her and said, "You don't know the half of it, Leah."

Leah shook her head. "You deserted them, John."

John's anger rose. "You think it's that simple? Fine! You try losing your best friend, then letting your team down."

Tears pooled in her eyes.

"I can't even look any of them in the eye anymore!"

Just then, the Irvington team jogged by. They stopped to see the commotion.

"Hey, look who we have here," Jim Patole said. "What happened Johnny boy, couldn't take the pain?"

The other boys laughed. John then pushed him so hard he went flying down to the ground.

"John!" Leah yelled.

The other boys stood in shock, unsure of what to do. Patole sat on the ground, staring at John, who was breathing heavy with adrenaline shooting through his veins. He looked like a wild animal ready to fight for its survival.

John noticed some adults approaching and took off. He ran to the other side of campus. He walked around the campus for a while and waited until all the people left before he went to the bus stop. His head was killing him.

When John got home, he went right to his mother's liquor cabinet where he found a full bottle of vodka. Before long, he was drunk and talking to himself. John stumbled into his room and looked at all the quotes and pictures of the runners on the wall.

"What do they know? So easy for them. So easy," John mumbled.

John put his hand over the poster. Then he snatched it from the wall and crushed it in his hand. "They think it's so easy," John kept mumbling. He ripped down another poster. When he was done with the posters and pieces of paper, he attacked the trophies, throwing each of them against the wall until they were smashed into pieces.

"Screw you! Screw all of you!" he screamed. When he was done with all the trophies and medals, he slammed his fist into the wall and made a huge dent. John kept hitting the wall until there were blood-stained holes all over.

Finally, the drunken well of self-pity passed out on the broken ruins of his dreams.

66

AT 9:30 A.M., THE DOORBELL rang. John tried to ignore it, but it wouldn't stop. Then someone started knocking at his window. John still did not budge. The window was slightly open and soon he heard his name being called.

"John? John? Are you in there?" Alex called.

"What?" he groaned.

"Can we talk?"

"No. Go away!"

"Come on, John. Let me in. I'm not going away until you do."

John stood up and opened his blinds to see Alex. He lay back down on his bed.

Through the window, Alex noticed the holes in the walls and debris all over. "Oh, my God, John! Are you okay?"

"What do you want?"

Alex took a moment, and then he said, "John, the season isn't over."

"What are you talking about?" John asked, perturbed.

"John, it's not over. We qualified and we need you for states. You can still run. I know you can do it."

John stood up and walked to the window. "My season is over, Alex." John pushed the window down and shut the blinds.

John lay in his bed after Alex left. He felt nauseous, and his head and hand were throbbing in pain. He finally found the energy to get some aspirin and ice, then lay down again.

John was unable to fall back to sleep. He kept thinking about how he let everyone down. At other points, he wondered about what Alex said. *Could he really run in the state meet? Was it possible?* No, there was no point, not with the way he had been running. He wouldn't even place in scoring position. *His season was over.* He had failed and failed miserably. Tears started to roll down. He cried through the pain and nausea he was feeling. He cried until he fell asleep.

Later in the afternoon he woke up. He felt somewhat calmer. The pain in his head and the nausea were gone, but his hand still hurt. John needed fresh air again, and some food so he got dressed and took a walk. It was cold, in the forties, and the sun was moving in and out from behind the clouds. John stopped at a deli for a big bottle of water and an egg sandwich. As he walked out, he bit into his sandwich. John finished half of it, and then threw the rest away.

He kept walking, taking in the fresh, cold air like it was his only source of life. John did not think about where he was going, he just kept walking into the cold breeze. He ended not far from the cemetery. He decided to enter.

John found Julian's grave. In a spontaneous act, he bowed in front of the tombstone and started to pray. He asked Julian and God for forgiveness. He prayed for help to mend his errors and right his course. He began to cry again. He stayed kneeling, crying and praying for forgiveness.

"John?" A familiar voice startled him.

His heart began to pound rapidly. He looked up to see Julian's mother standing next to him. John stood up. With a sad look in her eyes, she took John into her arms and held him tightly. She held him until the sobs stopped.

"It's okay, John. It's okay."

When she finally let him go, she spotted his raw and swollen hand. "What happened to your hand, John?"

He lowered his eyes.

"Let's take a walk."

Mrs. Seraphine held him as they walked. "You know, Julian used to get so nervous before his races."

"No he didn't."

"Oh, you're wrong. Nobody knows a boy like his mother. He hid it well, but inside he felt it."

They walked slowly. The cold breeze felt good against his face.

"You know he was afraid you were going to be better than him."

"What?"

"Yes. Oh, he'd kill me if he knew I was telling you this, but he was."

"Go on…please."

"He used to run in the mornings. He made me, his father and sister promise that we wouldn't tell you."

She chuckled and John smiled.

"But I think you both knew at the end."

She stopped and looked him in the eyes.

"He believed in you, John. I think even more than you believe in yourself."

She nodded at him to emphasize the point. And at that moment John noticed her eyes—they were Julian's eyes—and it seemed it was him speaking through her.

The message came all at once, like a great light illuminating his consciousness and penetrating to the center of his being. He had given in to his worst fears. John's deepest fear was that he was inadequate, that he was not as good as Julian and the others, and that he couldn't lead the team.

John had psyched himself out before the season had even started. Had he expected things to get easier as the season moved on? Had Julian still not trained harder than anyone else at his best?

Right there, at the cemetery, all the fears and illusions he had suddenly melted away. Everything became clear, and he knew exactly what he had to do.

Julian's mother dropped John off at home. He changed into his running gear so fast he almost fell over. John stopped himself by putting one of his hands on his thigh, which was as solid as a rock. It had been so long since he'd paid any attention to any part of his body. John went into the bathroom and looked in the mirror. He'd forgotten how solidly he was built. He remembered how much speed and power his body possessed. No part of him was undeveloped or weak.

Out he went into the biting dusk air.

John ran the loop he and Julian had run all summer. The last time he ran that loop was with Julian, the day before he died. The first few miles, his stride felt awkward and cold hair burned his lungs. But not long into the run, a wave of tranquility came over him and the pain left his limbs. The ground didn't feel as hard, and the cold air was not as harsh. He found strength and a source of energy that extended beyond the boundaries of his body. It was as if he was drawing in the energy around him and using that energy to propel him forward. As the run went on, he felt even more invigorated.

That night, John called Simon to apologize. John was surprised by his reaction. Simon immediately accepted it and did not even ask John to explain himself further. Afterwards, he called Leah. She wasn't as forgiving. She wanted John to get help, and told him she could not continue seeing him until he did so. John gratefully accepted her offer.

When he was finished, John did something he had not done in a very long time. He shaved his head.

Julian dragged John into the weight room one day after a particularly hard practice.

"What are you doing?" John asked.

"Working out," Julian said as he loaded the heavy plates onto the leg press.

John watched, astonished, as he did twelve repetitions. "That's more than the football players lift!"

"My legs are stronger than the football players' legs. Your turn," Julian said.

"I just did a workout, Julian."

"So did I."

"It's too much weight."

"Just do it!"

John sat down and took in a deep breath before he started. Every muscle in his body tightened as he did the first repetition, and he went again. His face turned red, with each contraction feeling like an explosion.

When he finished, John was met with Julian's smiling face. "First you don't want to do it and now it's a competition? You did 14."

"Oh," John said as he stood up.

Julian slapped him on the back before heading to the bench press.

67

MONDAY, JOHN FOUND DOWER AFTER school. He was sitting at his desk going through some paperwork. He looked like a true academic with his glasses on. John knocked on the door, even though it was open.

"Can I come in?"

"Sure," Dower said, not looking up.

"Coach, I need to talk to you." Dower recognized the urgency in John's voice and stopped what he was doing.

"What's going on, John?"

It was hard for John to get it all out, but eventually he did. Dower was patient, letting him speak, and not interrupting. John told him everything. He didn't see any reason to censor anything for Dower.

Dower told John he would do all in his power to get him help and assured him things would be okay.

"I'm sorry, Coach," John said. "I let the team down when you needed me."

"It's okay, John. You've been through a lot. But we are going to get you help. Things are going to be ok."

"Coach, one more thing. I want to run in the state meet."

Dower looked back surprised.

"You'll practice this week, then we'll make a decision."

Dower stood up. "Come on, let's go talk to one of the school counselors."

Dower put his arm around him as they walked down the hall.

"You finally cut that hair, huh, Bonds?"

John smiled.

68

WITH DOWER'S HELP, JOHN WAS able to put some of the pieces of his life back together. The school counselor called John's mom, and they had a meeting. John also told her everything. He thought he would be scolded by all three, but to his surprise they were compassionate and understanding. He would start an alcohol rehabilitation program and go to counseling. Given these conditions, he was allowed to continue training.

The final workout before the state meet was at Cedar Creek Park. The state course was hilly so Dower figured an extra hill workout couldn't hurt. The other guys were excited to have John back. They talked and joked during the run there.

On the first two intervals, John finished near the front of the group with Pedro or Simon. But on the third interval, he exploded in front of the others. By the end, he had a huge lead on the next man.

"Nice one, Bonds!" the assistant coach shouted.

Dower gave a nod of approval.

John led the next interval as well. Alex sat out the last interval as his Achilles tendon was still a little sore.

"Hey, Coach," Alex said as the boys ran their last interval.

"Yes, Alex," Dower said, staring out at his runners.

"Do you really think we can win the state meet?"

Dower didn't respond right away. "Stranger things have happened, Alex. Stranger things have happened."

69

THE STATE MEET WAS IN Poughkeepsie, which was a good five or six-hour drive away, depending on traffic. Normally, the team would be allowed to leave on a Thursday afternoon and have all day Friday to check out the course before racing on Saturday. But the assistant principal had planned his revenge well. He demanded the runners attend school on Friday.

Dower spent the afternoon arguing with the man, telling him how narrow-minded his decision was. He insisted that the team needed time to learn the course—especially in a meet of that caliber. He explained that if they waited until school was over, they would not reach the course until after dark. The coach felt it was not acceptable and potentially dangerous.

Dower's thirty years of tenure didn't win out, but the vice principal was forced to compromise. The team would have to attend a half day of school. This would still allow them to reach their destination before dark. Although Dower was dissatisfied, he knew when to quit, and agreed to it.

70

THE GRAY DAY SUGGESTED NOTHING but listlessness as the bus left Atlantic. But once they passed the city and headed further north, the dullness faded.

They went straight to the course when they arrived. It was a mild day for November and overcast. There wasn't much snow on the ground, just a few scattered piles.

As they ran the course, John didn't think it looked very tough—a few good inclines, but not enough to be labeled hilly. Overall, it looked like it would be a fast race.

That night, Dower took all the boys in his room for a pre-race speech. He warned them of who their enemies were, talked about race strategy and the weather forecast. The temperature was to drop overnight and the following day was going to be extremely windy. When he was finished with the serious business, he told them stories of past teams.

Unable to sleep, John lay awake for a long time that night. Then, as the nervousness gradually faded and sleep crept in, he noticed something. There was a part of the window where the shades did not meet. The sky had a hint of blue in it, even though it was nighttime. And it was in this small piece of sky where he felt a connection, an aura that connected him to all the runners from Atlantic's past. They were right outside his window, shadows and ghosts, peering in at him.

71

THE GIANT LOW PRESSURE SYSTEM that had brought overcast conditions the day before was a violent storm that had passed to the north of the region. Overnight, it exited into the Atlantic, dragging the veil of grey clouds with it. But it left behind a ferocious north wind and freezing temperatures. These conditions would favor the tougher runners.

Dower had a lightness to his step as he led the team to where they would set up camp. A group of the team mothers made the drive up. Julian's mother had come with them.

After the team warmed up, John did some strides on his own. The wind kept trying to veer him right, but he remained straight. When he finished, he looked around for the first time and really took in his surroundings. John stared at the myriad runners warming up on the yellowed field, the small mountains lining the distance, and the mammoth cloud formations. He could see and feel that winter was near.

A great presence suddenly came over John, silencing his thoughts. The events around him seemed to stop as he merged with it. In the silence, a deep unity was revealed between him and his surroundings and everything felt connected.

Not long after, the feeling was gone and his thoughts and vision returned to normal. John smiled. He smiled because everything finally made sense to him. He finally understood and completely accepted all the crazy events that had led him to that day. All the pain and suffering he had endured and caused others. It was simply the way things had to happen.

Then suddenly, Dower's voice boomed, "Atlantic runners, get dressed!"

John jogged to the camp and undressed to his uniform. Adrenaline began to pump fiercely through his system.

Dower brought them in to a huddle. His speech was short and to the point.

"This has been a long season for all of us. All the pain and suffering you have endured has brought you to this day, this moment. This is the end, but it is up to each of you to decide *how* it ends. Your goals and dreams lay right in front of you, but it is up to you to seize them. So go out there and do what you came here you to do."

"Final call, all runners!"

Julian's mother smiled at the team as they jogged past her towards the starting line. John saw her angelic face and dropped his gladiator stare for a moment to smile back.

The Atlantic team claimed its spot on the starting line. John remembered that Julian always lined up in the middle spot. He moved to the middle and inhaled deeply, once again noticing the presence.

"Runners, take you mark! Set!"

Boom!

The great line of runners converged towards a distant point, where soon, John's shaved head was visible not far behind the leader.

John went out fast, ahead of all his teammates. It was not the kind of race where the team could stay in a pack. Once he reached the front, he relaxed and decided to let a few runners pass.

The course was a giant loop so there weren't too many check points. The first one was less than a mile into the course. There was a lot of shouting as John passed, but he could make out Dower shouting, "Stay where you are! Don't let the leaders out of your sight!"

Dower offered encouragement to the others as they passed. After all the runners darted by, he tried to size up the situation with the assistant coach, but it was too early in the race to tell. They would have to wait it out.

The river of runners made their way into the back woods. At about the midway point it was John and five runners in a pack for the lead. John moved to the front and started to push the pace.

Not far back Pedro and Brett charged across the course. Simon and Alex were in back of them, but in sight.

Then suddenly, something John had not anticipated happened. Two runners with red jerseys from behind put in a huge burst and passed him. It was a little bit earlier than John had wanted to kick, but *it's now or never*, he thought.

The boys put in an impressive burst and did not waver. They were ahead of him as they reached the final check point.

"EVERYTHING YOU HAVE, NOW!" Dower yelled in a voice and tone reserved only for special occasions.

John's legs and stomach felt like they were being burned by molten lava. John closed his eyes for a brief moment to concentrate as the pain filled his body. The pain seemed to overwhelm him. Doubts filled his head. But then he focused his thoughts on Julian and what he meant to him. And Julian told him to give his all. Instead of resisting all the pain, he fully embraced it. He let the enormity of the brutal, fiery sensations engulf him. He moved in front of the two runners, immune to the cheers of the crowd. He ran the last straightaway in a near sprint, losing all form. But he kept his lead and crossed the line first.

John regained his senses just in time to see Pedro and Simon finish. They watched for the rest of the boys. Brett made an impressive kick and finished a few places ahead of Alex. Atlantic had placed its top five runners in the top 50 positions.

There were a lot of teams and it was hard to keep track of the scores, but Dower and the assistant coach tried their best.

"What did you get?" Dower asked the assistant coach as he put the pieces of paper next to each other.

"Ninety-six." they both said in unison.

The team stayed together near the finish line, and waited nervously for the scores to be calculated. Dower and several other coaches were huddled near the officials. Alex crept in behind them.

When the results were announced Dower made a vertical leap over a foot. Alex ran towards the others screaming, "We won, we won!"

Brett picked him up in the air as the others exploded in cheer. The others started screaming and cheering. They embraced each other and Dower. Some of them were even crying.

John walked over and gave Julian's mother a big hug. "That was for Julian," he whispered in her ear. She looked up and smiled at him.

After the meet, Dower took them out to a nice restaurant.

"Anything you guys want," he said. "Except beer."

The bus rolled home under a starlit sky with Brett happily taunting everyone by repeatedly playing "We Are the Champions" on his radio. Dower was too high on victory to mind or notice at first, but after an hour, and after many of the runners had threatened Brett's life, Dower used his hoarse voice to demand Brett shut it off.

Lowell's parents were away so he decided throw a party at his place that night. The entire cross country team and some other running friends, including the Baldwin team were invited. He had also invited the girl from camp with the American flag bathing suit, who he was now dating. The Baldwin guys got a kick out of that and paraded Lowell around as the guest of honor even though it was his house.

John's mom let him attend the party, only on the condition that she would pick him up at a reasonable hour and he not partake in any illegal activities. John also had asked her to pickup Leah and her friends. Leah promised John's mom that she would keep a close eye on him.

Later, while the party was still going strong, John looked for Simon. He had barely seen him all night. Finally, he found him standing on the deck without a coat. John grabbed his coat and headed out to join him. It was cold but a gorgeous clear night. Neither of them said a word and just looked up at the stars awhile.

"We did it, John" Simon said.

"Yeah, we did." John replied.

Then the screen door opened abruptly.

"Hey what are you punks doing?" Brett shouted. "Making out?"

They stayed up late, talking and laughing, stuck in their moment of triumph and glory.

72

THE NORTHEAST WAS THE MOST competitive division for cross country. And even though Atlantic was considered a big school, most of the schools they were competing against were much larger. At the Regional meet they were up against private schools too, notoriously known for recruiting kids, even though it was illegal and they had denied it. The only advantage the team had was that the meet was held at Van Cortland. They wouldn't have to travel and they knew the course well.

It was a mild day for November and there was almost no wind.

John's body and mind felt good as he warmed up. He had ample time to rest after states. Dower only gave them a few speed workouts to top off the grueling season.

Boom!

Not long into the race John knew something was off. It was only then he realized how much the race at States had taken from him. As he came down the final stretch in 16th place, Dower hollered with all the life in him. But John just didn't have it in him, and he missed qualifying for nationals by one place.

Pedro and Simon ran impressive times. Alex didn't run to his potential that day and Brett ran a horrible race. Lowell's time was consistent with what he had been running all season. Surprisingly, Benji was the fourth man. He came down the final stretch like a madman, passing five runners, finishing in record time for an Atlantic freshman.

Dower always said that cross country was the kind of sport where on any given day any team could win. Atlantic didn't win that day and none of the boys would be flying to sunny California to compete in the nationals. But one thing was clear: The group of hard-nosed kids from Atlantic proved not only that they could run with the best, but that they were contenders.

73

AFTER THE SEASON WAS OVER, a large awards dinner was held for all of the runners in the county. It was catered and held at a large hall.

John waited outside for Brett to pick him up. He put on his winter coat for the first time since last winter. He noticed it fitted him small and thought about getting a new one.

As they drove, Simon looked over his speech.

"Let me see," Pedro asked.

Simon handed him the speech, and Pedro read it and laughed.

"Shut up!" Simon said.

"Let me see!" Brett shouted at a red light.

Then Pedro handed it to him, and Brett laughed after reading it, too.

John grabbed it next and laughed as well.

"What is so funny?" Simon asked. But the only response he got was more laughter.

Inside, they were met with quite a reception. Runners and coaches came to their table all night, congratulating them. It felt weird, but John and the others began to enjoy it. Everything was going really smoothly until Brett got caught launching a dinner roll at the Irvington table.

"Brett!" Dower shouted.

After the first course and the introduction for the awards ceremony, John and the others camped out at Leah's table. When Leah got up to go to the bathroom, a few runners sitting nearby took the opportunity to go over and talk to him. He was shocked at how polite they were, not really understanding why they wanted to talk to him, and almost forgetting he was the state champion.

"Can we ask you some questions?" one of them asked.

"Shoot."

"Well, we hope to win states next season—what do you recommend?"

"Take out Alex and Benji."

Only one of the boys got the joke.

"I mean, how should we train?"

John thought about what to say—perhaps one of Julian's quotes he had read—but none of them seemed appropriate. Then something came to him, and he leaned over in his chair with his mean green eyes instilling fear and intimidation into the younger boys. "Do 1,000 miles over the summer."

They looked at him in awe. Then Leah came back and the boys took it as their sign to leave.

"Thanks, John." They said, shaking his hand.

"What was that all about?" Leah asked.

"Nothing." John waved his hand casually. "They just wanted to know the secret of cross country."

"Do tell."

"Well, it's simply a matter of mastering yourself."

Leah started laughing. "So you think you've mastered yourself?"

"Me? Nah, I'm just raw talent, baby." John pulled her onto his lap and gave her a kiss.

When the team was called up for their award, there was a huge round of applause as they made their way to the stage.

Dower made a very brief speech and ended with, "As far as I'm concerned, this is the toughest team I have ever coached." He moved out of the way to let Simon take the microphone.

Simon began fumbling through his pocket with one hand, then both. Simon looked around nervously. John and the others soon realized what the problem was and started laughing. Dower was confused and became impatient. What he didn't know was that Simon had lost his speech.

Finally, Simon grabbed the microphone. The laughter stopped and the room went silent when he began to speak. "I'd like to start by thanking everyone who supported us this season. We couldn't have done it without your help."

Dower put his hand on Simon's shoulder.

"I know a lot of you out there think you're different from us, but you're not," Simon continued. "Anyone can be great in this sport. Anyone."

There was a huge bloom of applause that turned into a standing ovation. Simon was so nervous he didn't even realize the profundity of his words.

John understood as he sat back down at the empty table and looked over the room. He watched the wandering eyes of some of the younger boys and girls, the camaraderie, the unspoken bond with everyone in the room. John knew there was something different about cross country runners.

While cross country was the epitome of a team sport, each runner was always alone. In all the grueling runs, practices, workouts, and races they were always on their own. The decision always came down to one person: The runner. The real enemy was not another runner or the team—it wasn't outside the runner. The real battle took place within.

At all times, the runner was responsible for taking himself to the breaking point of his own suffering and from there, he had to choose if he would keep going. He was the torturer and prisoner all at once, and he was always in control. It was like some grand game designed by a maniacal genius, almost too wild to comprehend, and it could only make John chuckle.

That night the Atlantic runners left alone and they also left together.

WINTER

It was not even six o'clock and the sun had drowned into the horizon with just a faint blue afterglow lingering. A thin lining of snow covered the ground and everything moved like shadows. Winter had arrived and seemed to be eternally present. All of the other seasons seemed forgotten and swallowed by the sorrowful, brooding landscape.

74

JOHN WOKE UP EARLY. IT was a Sunday, but he was unable to sleep late. He had left his blinds open and sunlight filled his room. He stood up and looked out the window. Fresh white, snow lined the ground.

He sat back down on his bed. He looked at the shelf opposite his bed. There were now medals and plaques all over it. Many first place wins, but also some second and thirds.

One medal in particular stood out. The medal from the state meet. He picked it up and looked at it carefully. It was nicer than all the other medals he had. But then a feeling of emptiness came over him as he looked at the shiny medal. He didn't like that medal. Even though it was nicer than all the other ones, it brought up too much pain. And even though he had earned that medal he would have rather not.

John dressed and walked outside. The cold air soothed him. The sky was a glorious blue with a few thin clouds. Although the fall was gone, it seemed too nice to be winter.

He decided to take a walk. As he walked, John took deep inhalations of the clean, pure air. He felt good. Things were starting to go well for him. He was getting help and everything in his life was getting better. He had repaired much of his family life and his relationship with Leah was blossoming.

John decided to stop by the cemetery. He had not been there in awhile, since the day of county meet. When he arrived he could tell no one had been there yet that day. The snow was fresh. He walked down the white road to Julian's tombstone.

John took a long moment to pay his respects to Julian. Then he went on his way, all seven medals embracing the tombstone.

Acknowledgments

I WOULD LIKE TO THANK all my friends and family for their love and support through this long ordeal. You guys never stopped believing in me!

I would also like to extend a special thank you to Jean Robin, my grandmother. Without you, grandma, this project may have never seen the light of day!

This novel was edited by Lissette Norman. I would also like to credit Carol Hoenig and Kay Sexton for their editorial contributions.

CPSIA information can be obtained
at www.ICGtesting.com
Printed in the USA
FFOW03n0323110416
23139FF